About the Author

Sylvia Webber has worked as a teacher and has brought up two children. She has written ‚*Her Story in Four Centuries, Rider the Runaway, What Narissa Did in the War* and *Traveling with Santa.*

Ayesha of the Poor and Persecuted

S M WEBBER

Ayesha of the Poor and Persecuted

NIGHTINGALE PAPERBACK

© Copyright 2024
S M Webber

The right of S M Webber to be identified as author of this work has been asserted by her in accordance with the Copyright, Designs and Patents Act 1988.

All Rights Reserved

No reproduction, copy or transmission of this publication may be made without written permission.
No paragraph of this publication may be reproduced, copied or transmitted save with the written permission of the publisher, or in accordance with the provisions of the Copyright Act 1956 (as amended).

Any person who commits any unauthorised act in relation to this publication may be liable to criminal prosecution and civil claims for damages.

A CIP catalogue record for this title is available from the British Library.
ISBN 978 1 83875 450 1

*Nightingale Books is an imprint of
Pegasus Elliot MacKenzie Publishers Ltd.*
www.pegasuspublishers.com

First Published in 2024

**Nightingale Books
Sheraton House Castle Park
Cambridge England**

Printed & Bound in Great Britain

In loving memory of my dear son Jason, 1966-2022.

CHAPTER 1

Ma sent Ayesha to sell the fish and to buy fresh fruit and vegetables after Dad left to go diving. Normally, Ayesha would have taken Dido with her, to carry things or mind the boat while she shopped. Ma couldn't accompany her because Grump was unsteady on his legs; Gran or Grump might have a fall or even fall into the sea and drown.

'You'll have to take the canoe on your own,' said Ma, 'and leave it at our jetty without a guard.'

There was a special jetty used by their group and their rights to it were generally honoured by the land dwellers.

'One of our neighbours might be there and could keep an eye on it,' said Ayesha. 'Or we will risk having it stolen.'

Ma shrugged. What else could they do.

Ayesha always loved paddling the canoe to the shore for the few minutes it took, and seeing what the weather was like, what the clouds and the surface of the sea looked like. Today, it was choppy, with a wind blowing against the tide, which made it harder and longer to reach the shore. The little waves with their lacy frills of spray were against her today.

She was feeling excited, like the choppy water, about finding the location of a literacy class she had heard of. She could only read and write a bit because her people, being stateless, were denied education. Her family were supporting her in her efforts. It would change her life.

She nosed the canoe between two larger boats at the jetty and tied it to a post. As luck would have it, her friend Odin was minding the boats today. At some distance, she only waved and pointed to the canoe. He looked up and nodded.

She had to leave the fish she wanted to sell in the canoe, because it was too heavy for her to carry to the market on her own. She had flounder and some rare abalone. She would bring the buyers around later. The jetty wasn't far from the market.

The walk to the market was along the waterfront. When she reached it, she was immediately delighted by a box of ripe mangoes that she would love to take home. In her anxiety to claim it, she tripped over it and some of the fruit fell out and split open. The owner of the mangoes screamed 'Watch out!' Other people turned to stare.

'I want to buy the box,' Ayesha said loudly.

The owner of the mangoes recognized her and said, 'Where is your money?'

A man called out, 'Sea gypsy!' and spat at her. Another man said, 'You smell, you beggar.'

There was nothing about Ayesha that suggested she was different from other people. She had the same dark hair and skin, with brown eyes. With her old but clean t-shirt and jeans, she seemed like any other teenager who roamed the streets of the town. But she was regarded as foreign, an intruder.

A school boy bent down, picked up a handful of gravel and threw it at her. This was what usually happened.

If one person said something rude about her, the others followed suit, supporting one another as a group. Sometimes, they spoke slowly and loudly as if she were deaf or stupid or couldn't speak the language properly.

Ayesha didn't actually have any money with her because she was aiming to sell the fish first. Or arrange a barter. Before selling, she'd come to see what fruit she could buy. When she didn't produce the money from her pockets, the growing crowd shouted, 'Shame, shame on you! You must pay for the mangoes.'

Often treated this way, Ayesha never got used to it. She reddened and said, 'I have to sell the fish in my canoe first.'

A man who had bought her fish before said, 'It is as she says. I'll come with you, Ayesha, to see and buy some of your fish today.'

He calmed down the owner of the mangoes and said he would guarantee their return shortly to pay for the fruit. The disturbance was thus resolved. Ayesha and the man walked to the canoe and he purchased all the catch. They returned together to the market. Ayesha bought the box of mangoes and the owner lent her a trolley, which the man vouched for. Ayesha procured some tomatoes and other vegetables and pushed all of it back to the boat. How she would have appreciated having Dido with her again, she thought.

Odin was still minding the boats. Sometimes, Yasmin took over from him. Yasmin was her and Odin's friend. She went to the market later in the morning than Ayesha. She was rather lazy and didn't get up early.

Ayesha wasn't ready to go home yet. She spread a tarpaulin over the fruit and vegetables and walked towards the town. She had learnt about a literacy class and wanted to investigate what she had heard. None of her people could attend school because they lacked citizenship, so they were illiterate. Ayesha had been meaning to try and learn to read and write for ages. Mainly because Dido had died, she resolved to go to the class for his sake. He would have wished for her to do it if she'd told him about it, and she might even have persuaded him to come with her. But she had done nothing, and now she was determined that would change. Life was too short to postpone what you must do.

Ayesha knew to go to the convent to ask about the class. She thought she could find the convent on her own and she did, because people had described it to her as an unusual, decorated type of building from the colonial times. Along the way, people kept directing her to it. She asked at the tourist information office. They told her she would know when she was nearly there by the old, cobbled street. She saw a straying cat and, disturbed by its mewing, bent down to stroke it; she loved animals. When she reached the convent, she knocked on the door and it was opened by a nun.

'I've come about the literacy class,' said Ayesha. 'I believe Sister Rosa runs it.'

'Yes, she does. Come in, and I'll see if someone can speak to you.'

Ayesha was ushered into a large entrance hall. The nun pointed to a comfortable chair she could sit in and went away. Ayesha waited a long time. It was lunchtime and she was getting hungry. At last another nun came, who said she was the manager and would make an arrangement for Ayesha over lunch. I'm glad about that, thought Ayesha.

Some nuns were seated around the table, talking quietly with one another. They gave a nod towards Ayesha as she sat down and continued with their conversations. Sandwiches and cups of tea were brought in by a nun.

The nun who was with Ayesha said, 'You can attend the young adult classes. Mostly the nuns are busy teaching school children, but Sister Rosa Ignatius does the ones for older teenagers.

'A Saint Ignatius founded our Jesuit order long ago, which is a very intellectual and learned one, interested in pedagogy. That means teaching, how to teach. Some of our classes are in the day, and some in the evening.'

'A day class would suit me better,' said Ayesha.

'The day class meets every weekday afternoon for two hours. Now, would you be able to pay for the class? I suppose not, as you seem to be a teenager.'

'I could not pay,' said Ayesha, turning red with embarrassment. 'We only make enough from fish to support our family of five.'

'That's all right. Any time you are able to donate something towards our good work, we would be most grateful to receive it. We're always in need of money. Or do a good deed for us. Have you learnt some reading and writing?'

Ayesha didn't like to say she'd learnt any reading and

writing and raise the nun's expectations of her. She knew the names of streets, traffic signs, numbers and such things.

'No.'

'How old are you?'

Again, Ayesha felt embarrassed. 'I'm not sure how old I am. You see, my mother measures my height every year at the time of a special celebration and makes a mark on the wall, but sometimes she may have forgotten to. Also, she measured my little brother too, in the same place, so sometimes the marks may have got muddled up.'

'Have you a rough idea of your age?'

Ayesha thought a bit. 'Yes, I think about sixteen, or maybe more.'

'That will do. Did you know, Jesus says, "Seek and you shall find, ask and you shall receive, knock and it shall be opened to you".'

'Oh, that's just what has happened to me.'

When Ayesha met Sister Rosa, the first thing Sister Rosa said to her was, 'People from any station in life are always welcome at the convent.'

Ayesha felt offended by what the nun said because she seemed to be calling her a beggar or some such thing, which people often called her in the street. Everyone reviled her people, calling them names and dirty and thieves. Sometimes, they begged from tourists, who took photos of them. So they were called beggars. Ayesha didn't disclose this to the nun; she thought, I'll tell her about it later when I know her better. Sister Rosa said to come to the class the next day. Some students had already begun it, but it wouldn't matter.

Ayesha went home and told Ma about her being accepted for the class. Ma already knew of her intention of finding out about it and she was happy for her to go. But Ayesha was still to take fish to the market first thing in the morning and come back later with the usual provisions every day of the week.

'Don't get into trouble with anyone.'

As if I would intentionally, thought Ayesha. It's other people who pick on me.

The next morning, she got into the canoe with her load. Waves were whispering to one another around the landing posts as she left. Gulls were wheeling and mewing. It was a calm day. The sea was flat but with dimples in it, almost like a mirror being tilted a little one way and then another.

At the jetty, Odin was there as usual. Ayesha lugged the fish, rather heavy as it was, in an old sack to the market. She was going to buy the other things later in the day. Without speaking to anyone, she laid out the fish on the ground, on the sack, and waited patiently for shoppers to purchase them. When she had sold all the fish, she walked to the convent to her class. After the class, she went back to the market to buy fruit, vegetables, rice, water and fuel before returning home.

On the way to the jetty, a man threw an old coat at her. Bearing the provisions, she had no hands to deflect it. It hit her, that object of charity as she was before it fell to the ground.

The man shouted, 'You damaged my mangoes. Watch

out!'

Ayesha walked on, eyes neither to the right nor left. Paddling home, she took heart from the phosphorescent lights in the water.

She said to her mother, 'Did I ever complain to you about how people at the market treat me?'

'No. Not that I can remember.'

'They revile me and call me nasty names because I am Bajau. It used to be better when Dido was with me because we seemed to support each other against their sneers and slights.'

'What do they say?'

'That we are beggars and the scum of the earth.'

'We know people say things about us, but not to children!'

'Well, they do, taking advantage of us.'

Ma was usually at home, she thought, away from it. 'I try to make it like water off a duck's back, but it still hurts.'

'Come and tell me every time it happens and we can share the burden.'

CHAPTER 2

Ayesha dived down to where Dido had died. She liked to go back there because her younger brother had been part of her life. She tried to experience the situation he had been in when he died. Dad was training him at that time. He had breathed in water by mistake. The water had gone into his lungs and he couldn't expel it without breathing in more. She was sure he would have tried to reach the surface of the water, but he couldn't make it. She dived down again to the place where he died, through the floating plants, to the seaweed, sea grass, corals and rocks of the ocean floor. This was his home.

Dad might have called to him but Dido couldn't hear him. His hands and cheeks had brushed against the rocks and seaweed and fish down there and he had found the entrance to Heaven. So, for Ayesha, this was where Heaven was, where all people went when they died, under the rocks and into the core of the earth where there was rock and fire, through this watery doorway. She wanted to retrace the journey Dido had taken, as far as she could. In her mind, she called out to him as she stroked the rocks and seaweed. She imagined he might hear her and feel comforted by her voice. He would know she had not forgotten him and that he was still part of their family and loved. She would never stop making these journeys and never forget him.

Of course, Dad went there every day spearfishing and gathering shellfish and looking for pearls, and Dido would be aware of his presence. They were a family who lived close to Heaven, with their goodness and purity, and that was true. It was Heaven for their tribe.

Dido became part of the watery world he went to, eaten, as he was, by fishes and other animals. His spirit went into them and into the ground where he fell. He was everywhere down there. That was what Heaven was like, where the entities merged into one and ultimately into the One that was God. That was their life everlasting – it couldn't be destroyed. They were being eternally reincarnated.

Dad wanted to put a gravestone for Dido on the sea floor. But really, it was full of rocks, and what they needed was someone who could carve a memorial to Dido into the rocks. They couldn't because they couldn't read and write. One day, she would learn to do it. Dido would have wanted her to learn to read and write. She would do it for his sake.

After Dido died, Ayesha sometimes talked or whispered to herself when she was alone in their shared room because she had been used to talking with him. Or she talked to him directly. Dido had had a pet tortoise, the only pet they'd ever kept, and sometimes he'd dive into the ocean to rescue it, as it wasn't an ocean-going tortoise. After he died, Ma, Asmida, gave the tortoise away to some friends.

Dad, Bulan, built their house. It was one of fifteen huts in a group. It was called a stilt house because it was firmly attached by stilts to the sea floor. The house was made of water-resistant bamboo and timber, and the floor was above the water at high tide. Sometimes, water came up into the floor in a storm. The roof was sloping, finished with corrugated metal.

Dad made their boats. There were two of them, both dugout canoes hollowed from a tree trunk. Sometimes, he got jobs making or mending other people's boats. Some of their people lived in houseboats he had helped to build and sailed between countries. If Dad needed any assistance, he could count on someone else in their group.

In the large living room of their house, it seemed Ma was always cooking meals on the open wood fire on a sheet of metal in the centre of the floor. There was no electricity and you lit a hurricane lamp at night. No telephone. The meals were mostly fish, and cassava, porridge made from a root vegetable. Sometimes, they ate seaweed. Ma was responsible for cooking, housework, washing, mending, hand-sewing and care of the children. Ma didn't do a lot of cleaning because she said it was mostly 'clean dirt'. After all, it had been washed by the sea.

Ayesha's room was off the living room, and you had to walk through it to Ma and Dad's room, so people were always walking across her room and trespassing on her right to privacy. When Gran and Grump came to live with them, Dad built a room for them on part of the landing, so that you could walk past their room into the living room without intruding on them. The landing continued like a veranda down another side of the living room.

At the landing where the boats were moored was a ladder up from the water; just logs of wood. Sometimes Ayesha would lie on the veranda part of the landing, thinking, and looking up at the scudding clouds; pretending that the clouds were still, and watching the earth seeming to go round.

Ma was kind but sometimes acerbic. She would say, 'If you go on making that face, the wind might change and you'll be stuck with it forever.' She always said, 'There's no such word as can't', and she thought that illness was caused by the mental state of the person. Dad was mostly at work; at home he was jolly, like Santa Claus, even though he was tired from all the physical work he did in the day.

Grump was often grumpy. Gran was sometimes a bit sharp or snappy. She had a scratchy voice. She walked around talking to herself, so people had to ask her whether she was talking to *them.*

Dido had been noisy and bouncy, rushing about the house. Mum and Ayesha said it caused the house to rock and sway slightly in the ocean. Dad said it did *not.* Sometimes, when the dishes fell down, he said it might be a spirit.

In the house, you could hear the whispering of the waves and creaking of poles. Ayesha recalled how Dido, as a baby, slept in a hammock strung from the ceiling. People gave the hammock a little push to rock it, as they walked back and forth in the living room, or any time Dido cried.

The cracks between the wooden floorboards created

lines of bright blue. Dido had sat cross-legged over the cracks and dropped a line through them. His lure was a piece of flounder skin. He sometimes hooked an eel and pulled it up through the crack. It twisted around like a snake! Everyone would scream and jump back, pretending they were frightened. Real sea snakes were venomous.

Ma washed their clothes and sometimes they all just jumped into the water with their clothes on. The washing was strung out along the landing and down the veranda. Ayesha washed her own underwear and was appointed to clean the dishes. They bathed and washed their hair in the sea. They dumped their garbage in the sea. Their squatting toilet off the landing emptied into the sea. The fish ate the refuse. Then they expelled it, and so on. The sea converted all their waste into food for living things.

It was a canoe ride of a few minutes to the shore to take fish to the market and buy the provisions every day. At low tide, you could walk the distance with water up to your neck. Canoes went back and forth between houses, children chattering aboard. The sea and the boats were the playground for children. They all learnt to swim very young. You watched them swimming in the water like dancers. They never came home empty-handed, learning to be hunters of the sea.

Ayesha mused, Imagine you are a sea anemone waiting for a small fish to come – have you ever put your finger in one and felt it try to suck it in? When you came, Dido, you put a finger on my heart and touched it, and my tentacles were out waving and welcoming you. I am like a rock in the sea with soft things clinging to it or nestling there.

Now I see Dido's face just under the water, the moment before he surfaces and takes a deep breath. His face is rippled and wondering, as if he is being born. A bubble of air comes up from his mouth – is it his first or last breath? Will he go under again, like someone who is drowning? But then his face rises out of the water, ringed by its edge, and he takes a deep breath.

We all come from the sea, she is our mother, Mother Ocean; the land is a father. With her cycles, the ocean is where man is closest to woman. He dives into her and she envelopes him, or she is lapping on the shore, a bridge between two worlds.

The moon is a mother, making the tides; the sun a father, making plants grow. If I am restless in the night, or have pain from my period, I get up and go to sit on the veranda. I look up at the full moon, which is synchronized with my period; everything is working together in nature. The Moon Spirit has Ma's face looking down at me and smiling. If I am walking along, the moon follows me.

Dad often calls me his princess. He always makes me feel special. So I am used to being the princess Ayesha. Her reincarnation. I had a dream in which I was the incarnation of Princess Ayesha. She was on her way to be married to a ruler but was swept away by the sea. Her father, the king, sent a child to search for her, and that child started our tribe. From then on, the sea gave us all we would ever need. We became hunters of the ocean.

Ayesha explained to land dwellers that were interested: Dad and the divers wear wooden goggles with lenses made of scrap glass, a diving mask and handmade fins on their feet. They have weights to pull them down. In the water at the edge of a reef – where you can drink the water – are sea urchins at full moon at a low tide, giant clams, scallops, coral fish and sea cucumbers. With heads half-submerged, the divers scan the sea, gauge the depth, spot a fish – maybe an octopus – take a breath, reach for a spear, dive in and spear it. They look out for deadly sea snakes.

After diving finishes, they decompress their ears by leaning their heads back and looking up. They rarely dive if it is raining. Rain affects visibility; there is less light and the rain carries mud and sediment. There could be wind and rough waves. Entry and exit could be difficult, even impossible. So they stock up on fish for a rainy day.

Our people lived the same way from time out of mind of humankind. We can't read or write and are stateless, without rights to education, health care or social services. If we are sick, the hospitals won't accept us – we might get arrested. Yet we are cheerful, hospitable, not aggressive to other people and believe in the equality of all:

CHAPTER 3

When Ayesha first arrived at the literacy class, Sister Rosa welcomed her, gave her a pen, a pencil, an exercise book, some work sheets and a copy of the Bible, which she said was the textbook and was free. She showed her to a small desk at the front. Ayesha observed her closely and saw an old woman, short of stature, with narrow eyes and heavy dark eyebrows. She was stooped and her hands trembled.

Shushing the other students, Sister Rosa introduced her: 'Ayesha is joining us a bit after this class began the course, but she will do catch-up work on her own and participate in class discussions. She can read and write English a little and speaks it well, I think.'

She is being kind to me, thought Ayesha.

Sister Rosa then introduced some of the students sitting near to Ayesha. Gideon was Jewish. His father had come to the town as a rabbi. Gideon had been brought up in Israel speaking Hebrew and hadn't learned much English at school. The twins, Sun Yat-sen and Han Suyin, named after famous people, but usually called Sunny and Hannah, were half-Chinese and half-Australian. They normally lived in a country town in China where their father was in business, and only spoke limited English because their mother was used to speaking Mandarin. They were Buddhist as their mother believed in a form of

Buddhism she had learnt about in Western culture, which was different and sometimes conflicted with their father's view of it. Noor was Muslim and her father was a foreign anthropologist, a person who studied cultures, working in the university. Other students in the class were Christian, agnostic and atheist. Tomasin was American and a Protestant. Her father was working for the government. Jake was English. Ayesha got a general idea of it.

At this point, Jake spoke up and said, 'I was brought up as a Christian, but actually I don't believe in God. I tell people I'm agnostic because I can't be sure, and I know this reply won't offend them. I also think atheists often hate religion and religious people in a way I do not. Jesus was a real person, his story is true, except for the miracles. Even if God exists, I'm sure there isn't life after death, but you just lose consciousness. There is no logical reason why you have to believe in life after death because you believe in God.'

Sister Rosa said that life after death was written in the Bible, and it was good to hear from Jake at last what he thought, as he had not been forthcoming up to now.

Gideon and the twins had red hair with fair skin and freckles. Gideon said Jewish children were usually dark, but some were like him. The twins said Chinese people never had red hair and they had called Europeans 'Red devils'. They had inherited red hair from their mother. People stared at them. They were wearing caps saying, "Hat Head", a place in Australia. Their aunt had sent them. Noor wore a black headscarf.

While the class was writing a composition, Sister

Rosa took Ayesha aside and said, 'I want you to select one of these pictures I cut from old newspapers to take home and write something about the picture, if you can. Bring it back whenever you've finished. Don't worry about making mistakes.'

She told all the students, 'I've given this speech earlier to the class, but since then some new students have enrolled, so I'm repeating it.

'I will give you homework to do, and it's up to you then. It's not compulsory to come to this class. If you've had enough, you can leave. You can come back, also. If you don't like what I'm teaching, you can bring it up for discussion in class. I may change it slightly on the advice of all the students.

'I have to make up my own teaching materials. If you want to present any material to the class of your own, I'd be delighted. You should tell me about it first. The class can go offsite as a group to visit or inspect something of interest – any suggestions?'

She paused for the students to respond, but there was only a low buzzing; a sort of 'maybe' or 'we'll think about it'. Sister Rosa then began to cough and sneeze a great deal so that she couldn't continue speaking but held onto the side of the desk with one hand, cupped the other over her mouth and rocked as she coughed.

Quiet as she could, Hannah, who was nearest to Ayesha, said, 'She has heart failure. It doesn't mean her heart is going to fail any minute, though you might think so, but only over a long time, as she has explained to us.'

After Sister Rosa had blown her nose, wiped her eyes

with a tissue and recovered her ability to speak, she went on, 'When we speak a language, there isn't a right or wrong way to do it. People have different accents. Their grammar isn't perfect. They might put words together in ways unfamiliar to others, especially if they are speaking, for them, a second language. Anyone might not speak in proper sentences. As long as you can be understood you are communicating, and that's all that matters. If you don't understand someone, tell them. As you learn to write a language, you will learn correct formal language and how to write sentences.'

Sister Rosa turned her back to write on the blackboard, and Ayesha saw a student throw a piece of paper shaped like a plane at someone, who unfolded it and was reading something written on it, and another student was whispering to someone else. Sister Rosa ignored these things. She didn't treat them like children – they weren't mucking up.

She turned around, causing the students to sit up straighter and pay attention. She said, 'I'm giving speaking its place in this course because it's important to learn to speak well and be a confident speaker. Also, being aware of how you speak helps you to learn to read and write. They all aid one another.

'I'm only qualified to teach Christianity, and you'll be getting plenty of that. I'm biased in doing that. Apologies if anyone's offended. But I don't teach you to belong to a particular church.'

'I should think not,' said Tomasin.

Ayesha thought that was rude.

Sister Rosa reminded the students about the school library where they could sit and read quietly or borrow books. They could book a meeting room next to the library to hold their own discussions in. She would host a get-together for the students once a year.

Jake put up his hand. 'Can we book the meeting room now and have a regular booking?'

'Yes. Would other students agree to that?' A number of students put up their hands. 'You can have it on late Friday afternoons after the class.' There were several yesses, and Sister Rosa recorded the booking.

At the end of the class, the students told Ayesha that Sister Rosa was not sharp-tempered, in spite of her weasel look. She always did what she said she would do and went charging on at it with an indomitable spirit.

Ayesha lay awake that night thinking about everything that had happened. She had many hours to fill in a day because she wasn't going to school. Sometimes, she would talk in her mind to her namesake, the princess of long ago. She would ask the princess what occurred after she left her father to go to the ruler she was to marry.

'I suppose, unlike me, you learnt to read and write as a young child. I'm now catching up at an older age,' she told the princess.

Princess Ayesha said, 'I will tell you my story. I was the daughter of a king who ruled a kingdom of which the people were land dwellers. As a child, I had tutors who came to the castle to teach me to read and write and do numbers. Then I studied all the normal school subjects. I was also taught how to behave as a princess should. I thought I was good at everything because others always praised my efforts, and I looked down at ordinary folk, which was not surprising in my station in life.'

'You came from a high station in life,' said Ayesha, 'but I came from a lowly one.'

'Maybe, but a time was to come when I would change all my highfalutin opinions because of the circumstances I was in. My parents would try to force me to marry a man of rank without my consent and without my even getting to know him.'

Ayesha yawned. This is becoming complicated, she thought.

The princess said, 'I'll go on with my story another time.'

Ayesha fell asleep.

On the following Friday, the students went to the meeting room to have discussions. The chairs felt comfortable. At first, having been suddenly thrust into the situation, no one could think what to say. So, Sunny began to talk with Hannah in an entertaining way. It was just like twins to talk to each other. Sunny described a huge statue of a past leader in China, with live pigeons pecking at something, and crapping, on his head. A traffic policeman was standing at the base of the statue directing the traffic.

'It was very comical. The arms of leader and the policeman were similarly placed, one arm held up and the other pointing to the side.' His mother had taken a photo of it.

Hannah said, 'Mum took a photo in a Muslim country we were visiting once of a woman in purdah, all black, carrying a plastic bag full of cigarettes. The bag was bright red, with a picture of a Marlboro man on horseback smoking a cigarette on it. It struck me as amusing - the incongruity of it.'

Jake said, 'I wish I'd taken a photo of something once. I saw a row of little birds sitting on the edge of part of a birdbath, all chirping excitedly. One of them took a bath at a time while the others watched. They were very sweet.'

'When I was travelling on a train in China,' Sunny went on, 'a woman was in charge of boiling water in a large canteen standing on the floor, which she would pour into flasks in each compartment. There was supposed to be enough water to last to the next stop. But when it ran out, she went around every compartment and shared out the water that was left – some still had water. This shows she had Marxist beliefs, *'From each according to his ability, to each according to his needs.'*

'I don't think that's necessarily true,' said Hannah. 'She was just sharing it – anyone would have done that.'

'Well, perhaps it shows that Marxism is based on what people naturally do.'

'I've just thought of another story,' said Hannah. 'I was trying to buy some cigarettes. By the way, I don't smoke any more. There was a woman sitting on a stool in the street selling them. The cigarettes were called 999. I said, "Why are they called 999?" She said in English, "Big heavy nines" – they speak English when they hear a foreign accent.

'I suppose 10 would have used up too much space on the packet, and they were "big heavy", meaning "very,

very" – here "good" is understood – a normal kind of expression in Asian countries, where people say "lovely, lovely girl" for "very lovely girl".'

The other students appeared to be stunned into silence. Then Noor said, 'I'm not allowed to travel long distance on trains on my own.'

'I don't have holidays in exotic countries,' said Tomasin.

'What's Marxism?' said Ayesha. At least I remembered the word, she thought.

Another student said she was a Marxist and appreciated what was told.

The twins said that some of the stories were their mother's. Being Australian, she liked travelling. As no one else made a similar contribution to the entertainment, the students started chatting on more mundane subjects. Jake and Tomasin explained that their reason for doing the class was social, as they were taking a gap year from schooling, being home-schooled. Shortly, a loud bell reminded them they were in a convent and it was time for the nuns to attend prayers, and the library, where the meeting room was, would be closing in five minutes.

On the way home, Ayesha noticed a young man on the side of the street by the waterfront near the jetty, leaning on his motorbike and watching cars and people go by. He was smoking a cigarette and looked her up and down as she came walking past. She halted to pat a dog to avoid his gaze – it didn't bite her – and asked him his name.

He said, 'Jihad. Jihad Jim they call me. My real name is James, but I'm always Jihad now.'

He didn't ask her name and she went on walking.

CHAPTER 4

One evening after Ayesha enrolled in the literacy class, a man came up to her at the jetty when she was carrying provisions and on her way home.

He said, 'You do dynamite fishing, and our group is going to bomb your house out of the water. Dynamite fishing damages fish and coral reefs.'

'My group don't do it.'

She got into the canoe quickly and left.

She went to the convent library after the market until her class began in the afternoon. The teacher-librarian told her she could sit and read and work on anything she had with her in the library, as well as borrow books and take them home to read. She could book time on the computer too. A librarian would show her how to use it at the simplest level.

A boy sitting at one of the tables saw Ayesha and called out, 'You lot are destroying the fish stocks, my father told me.'

'My family aren't,' said Ayesha. Not again, she thought.

The librarian told the boy, 'You are not allowed to be disrespectful to people in this library. The next time you do this, I'll send you out.'

The librarian helped Ayesha with her lessons. She

explained, 'You have an easy reader here for children. It says, "Molly picked some flowers in the garden". Sister Rosa has given you a question on your worksheet which says, 'What did Molly pick in the garden?" You must work out the answer and write it in the box here. You can check if your answer's right in the back of the worksheet. This one's number two. Do you know numbers?'

'Yes.'

'If you get the answer wrong, look back at the story to see how it happened. Don't be discouraged. People who are learning are bound to get something wrong now and then.'

Ayesha found out about Sister Rosa in the library. She was named after a distinguished Sister Rosa Ignatius of long ago who had devoted her life to the education of girls and women, especially poor ones, by setting up schools for them at a time when there were none for women so that they missed out on an education. But Rosa was the actual given name of their Sister Rosa.

Ayesha thought, I'll finish the easy readers as soon as I can, and then I'll read these library books the children are reading. For lunch, she just ate some carrots and tomatoes she had bought at the market. She took the time for her class from a wall clock, but later she acquired a cheap watch.

The class were reading the parables of Jesus. Sister Rosa often made students read from the Bible aloud in turn, an old-fashioned practice. She said they would find the parables relevant to their own lives. She read the parable of the sower to them, saying that it was about a farmer sowing seed to grow a crop, which was done by hand in those days.

'Who would the sower be?' she asked. 'You can join in this, Ayesha, as you have read it with me earlier.' She was paying special attention to Ayesha because she was new to the class.

Ayesha said, 'I think the sower could be anyone, not necessarily the farmer. The parable shows that where you sow seed matters. The person who sows seed by the wayside is careless in life, so what they do is wasted. The people who sow their seed on stony ground don't watch what they're doing so they might do things that are not very fruitful. Those who sow their seeds in thorny bushes can't see their own worth and spoil what they do.'

'Thank you for your long interpretation, Ayesha. You recognize some of the abstract meaning of the story. You have done well with no written notes. Anyone else?'

Gideon said, 'The seed is the word of God. The ground is the people. The seed falling by the wayside means some people hear the word of God, but don't understand it. The seed cast in stony places means the person is happy to receive it but has nowhere for it to take root. The seed cast among thorns means that the person's choice of a materialistic lifestyle, with its cares, prevents them from making any use of it. But the good ground means the person understands the word so that it grows and bears fruit. This is difficult stuff.'

'Thanks, Gideon. I think you are indebted to the Internet – good. The seed also represents the Gospel, the sower is the one who proclaims it, and the different grounds represent people's responses to the Gospel.'

'So the story can be interpreted in various ways?'

'It can.'

Tomasin said, 'Thus, it means the person who—'

'Help, help! I'm drowning in words,' said Ayesha. She looked around the room for support.

'My brain is tired out by it all,' said a student.

'I agree,' said Ayesha. 'What about the seed a man puts into a woman with his penis to grow a baby.' Some students giggled. 'Does the Bible have anything to say about it?'

'Yes, it does, but we haven't come to it yet,' said Sister Rosa. 'School children usually learn about it in sex education first.'

'I learned about it from Ma.'

'That's the best way. Now, we must get on. Did anyone read the parable about the seed growing secretly?'

'Not the seed again,' murmured some students.

Why is she so driven? thought Ayesha.

But Noora put up her hand to say, 'The seed grows even when the farmer sleeps. I suppose it means God, not humans or the seasons, determines the growth of living things.'

'Yes, the seed is the kingdom of God itself. And the parable of the mustard seed portrays a small seed which grows into a larger plant. It shows the kingdom of God can grow from small beginnings.'

'Excuse me,' said Jake. 'The seed or the baby grows because of nature, not God.'

'From your point of view, it does,' said Sister Rosa. '*I*

believe they are both involved.'

Sister Rosa gave the students homework to write about the parables that were discussed in class. She said, 'Say what you think and be critical.' As Ayesha wouldn't be able to do this, Sister Rosa said she would spend time reading the parable of the talents with her. A talent was a piece of money.

The next time the class met, Ayesha said, 'In the parable of the talents, I'm worried about the interpretation of "To those that have shall be given, and from those that have not shall be taken away even that which they have". If you were a Christian, why would you give more to those who have, and take everything away from those who have not? I'm interested in it because of my own people, who are the losers.'

Sister Rosa said, 'The meaning is that those who are open to God's advice will profit from it spiritually, and those who shut it out will have no benefit. He who understands will go on to understand more and receive the fruit of eternal life, while he who understands nothing will receive nothing and even his life will be taken from him.'

'That seems a bit harsh to me.'

'Look, the master put his servants in charge of his goods while he was away. On return, he checked to see how they acted. Two servants had invested his goods and turned a profit for him but the third had not, so he had to pay his master a fine,' said Sister Rosa.

'I don't think he should have fined the third servant. After all, the servant looked after the goods and caused no damage.'

37

The students knew they could go to Sister Rosa if they had any personal problems they wished to discuss. She could be found in her office. Ayesha decided to tell Sister Rosa about how she had felt offended by being named as someone of a 'low station in life'. She knocked on the door a few times. At last, it opened.

Sister Rosa said, 'Come in. I must have fallen asleep in my chair.'

Ayesha sat down on the spare chair, and said, 'I want to discuss what you said to me when I first met you. You said that people from a low station in life are welcome here. I am one of those people who have been made to feel inferior because I am Bajau. I don't like feeling I'm here out of charity. We are reviled and called beggars, which we are not.'

'People are certainly wrong to revile you, as Jesus would have said, and I'm sorry to have caused you offence.'

'Thank you. I know you didn't mean it. Since coming here, I've been becoming more critical and confident, so I see more clearly the discrimination against my group is undeserved. It hasn't taken long for these feelings to rise up in me. We are good, kind people who make a living and are not dependent on your society. They choose to call us beggars because tourists throw coins into the water to watch our children dive for them! If any of us are actually begging in the street, there would be many others doing it too.'

'A great writer said, "It is most miserable to feel

ashamed of home". I can see you are dealing with this problem as best you can. Jesus says to love even those who harm you and, if they strike you on one cheek, turn the other cheek to them. I suppose that would be difficult for a young person to do.'

'Well, I will try to live up to this standard then because of my namesake, Princess Ayesha, who founded my tribe.'

'Good for you! Do you have any other issue – something that's upsetting you?'

'I don't think so really.'

'Everything okay at home?'

Ayesha hesitated. She knew she could say anything. 'My young brother died recently from drowning. We are all feeling it still.'

'Oh, I am so sorry. My father died when I was your age and it made me feel like going into the church.'

'Well, I always have a runny nose since then and my mother thinks I have an allergy. I think I'm crying inside and I often have what I call "tears behind the eyes", which is what you feel when someone tells you a very sad, true story.'

'Would you feel better if you did drawings or write about it? It's a process of saying goodbye. Forgive yourself if you feel guilty in any way.'

'I just imagine it again and again. Sometimes, I talk to my brother and go down to the sea floor to visit where he drowned. It is his graveyard.'

'You know best what to do. You are doing well, Ayesha.'

When Ayesha saw Jihad again with his motorbike in the same spot near the jetty, she said, 'Do you always stand here as if you are waiting for someone?'

'I guess I do mostly.'

'What are you waiting for?'

'I pick up jobs this way.'

'Do you remember me?'

'No.'

'I think you do.'

After she got home, she found Ma had kept some food for her. Ma was still up.

Ayesha said, 'We hardly speak to each other any more. I come home ready to drop into bed with exhaustion and have to make myself eat some food first. In the morning, I'm in a rush to get away, gobbling down my breakfast with my mouth full!'

'It's all right, Ayesha. We want you to have this opportunity for education. Who knows where it might lead. You fulfil your responsibilities at home by taking the fish to market and bringing back necessary provisions. We are grateful for it.'

CHAPTER 5

Sister Rosa's heart failure meant that she sometimes ran out of breath. It was frightening. Would she collapse? When she came to, she cleared her throat with an awful barking noise like a seal. She coughed. She sneezed. Her sneezing was tumultuous. Ayesha started counting the number of times she sneezed in a row, and the record so far was eight. The sneezing wasn't related to heart failure, she thought, but might be due to old age.

As a nun had asked *her* what her age was, she said, 'How old are you, Sister Rosa?' But she wouldn't tell.

People said to the students, 'You have a wonderful teacher.'

They said, 'Yes, but we don't tell her that enough and should do it more.'

When class started again, Sister Rosa said, 'Can anyone think of something like this in their own life? The parable of the tenants is about how the kingdom of God was for those who produced good fruits. The tenants had the opportunity to live decently but they were ruthless and heartless. The tenants had totally rejected God, and goodness. To believe in God is to follow his will. A person cannot be on his own a perfect basis of faith, but only in God.'

Gideon said, 'In Israel, young people living in a

kibbutz often don't look after their buildings, or the gardens where they grow vegetables to sell. The fault is in *giving* them things. Young people need to work for what they have and then they will respect it.'

Ayesha said, 'My people are like the good servants, and all those, and there are many, who ill-treat them are like the wicked tenants.'

Sister Rosa said, 'Here's the parable about the prodigal son. I think it will ring a bell to some of you. A man had two sons. He divided his estate equally between them on request of the younger son, who travelled to a distant country and wasted all his money. He was forced to work.

'He thought, I will go to my father and say I have sinned and am not worthy to be called your son, so make me one of your servants.

'When his father saw him again, he had compassion and ran and embraced his son who had returned. He killed a kid for a feast, but the older son said, "I have served you and have not transgressed and you never gave me a feast."

'The father said, "It is appropriate we make merry and be glad, for your brother was lost to us and is found."

'God is merciful and gives time for reformation. Does this remind you of anything in your life?'

Several boys put up their hands.

'Yes, Jake?'

'My older brother went travelling; granted, with money he earned by doing temporary work in the holidays. He travelled cheaply, and when he came home, our parents were glad to see him safe and sound. He'd run completely out of money. He owed some money to people when he went away and knew they would want it repaid soon. He never should have borrowed it in the first place. So, our dad said he would pay off his loans for him. Our parents threw a party to welcome him, and he went back to living rent-free at home. Of course, I understand we are both still growing up and making mistakes.'

'Your story is apt. Jesus says God is putting forward love and graciousness over the law, merit or reward. This is the same belief that Jews have.' She nodded towards Gideon.

Sister Rosa then said she had a story to tell about the parable of the wheat and the weeds.

'In my church, we deal with all kinds of people. Some come to us to confess their sins. We listen and assign them an appropriate penance. These people don't always reform themselves immediately. They return again and again telling us their wrongdoings. They are like the evil people, in the parable, who sowed weeds. But we don't go around pulling up the weeds straight away, as it may harm others. We give people time to mature, and rarely excommunicate them. We leave that to God at the Last Judgement.

'As Jesus says, "He who has ears to hear, let him hear".'

'As a Protestant, I don't believe in excommunicating people,' said Tomasin.

Ayesha said, 'I learned about turning the other cheek from reading the parable of the good Samaritan with Sister Rosa. In this parable, a Jewish traveller is stripped of his clothing and beaten and left for dead by the side of the road. Passers-by, in turn, avoid him. A Samaritan comes along and helps the man, even though Samaritans and Jews despise each other. The parable answers the question "Who is my neighbour?" A neighbour is one who shows mercy to an injured person. I see that turning the other cheek is a part of loving my enemies. This can help people to live in peace and love.'

'Hear, hear,' said Tomasin.

Sister Rosa told them all to find more parables they could relate to.

The next time the students had a Friday meeting, they had thought up jokes and funny stories to tell. Ayesha said that the classes were giving her words to say things she hadn't said before. Noora brought tea, coffee, sugar and powdered milk, with biscuits. There were cups and spoons in a cupboard, an urn they could use and a sink with running water in the room.

'These biscuits we call "squashed flies biscuits" at home,' said Noora. They were flat ones with raisins in the middle.

Hannah said, 'About the prodigal son story, were the sons treated fairly? I think favouritism was shown to the prodigal one. I'm not always treated fairly at home. My mother expects me to be a certain kind of woman and my father worries about my relations with men. They don't treat Sunny the same way – he'll just go to uni and get a professional job and have whatever relations with women. Why can't they see me in the same way?'

'It's the relations with men,' said Sunny. 'They imagine you might come off worst in a relationship and it will pull you down in life. That's a realistic view.'

Noor said, 'My mother expects me to be high-achieving at uni, but that my Muslim background will guide me in other areas.'

'My mother and I are always arguing, I mean fighting,' said Tomasin. 'She can't just let me be myself but is highly opinionated about what I should be and do. Always making judgements and saying what ought to be. She gets my goat.'

Gideon said, 'Well, my father expects me to be very good in everything. My mother just goes along with it.'

'The same for me,' said Jake, 'and I have sometimes let Dad down. But he has the English stiff upper lip and bears it stoically.'

'What can we say about all this?' said Ayesha. 'You can't assume that parents are just what you want them to be. They have different personalities and views from you. Go on sticking up for yourself and becoming independent.'

'Thank you, Sister Ayesha,' said Jake.

Before they left, Noor invited Ayesha to come to her place one morning, and chat and do some things. Ayesha was delighted. She wondered if Noor would like her. Noor explained how to get to her house.

When Ayesha arrived, Noor said, 'Dad asked me if I could find time to do some digging in the garden, for putting vegetables in later. I thought I would like help from someone I'd like to talk with while we did the job.'

'I've never done gardening,' said Ayesha. 'I'd like it very much.'

Noor showed her how they had to dig the soil, turn it

over and break up any sods. There wasn't enough soil in the vegie garden, but there was some banked up in another part of the garden which they could bring over in the wheelbarrow.

'It's quite hard work,' said Noor, as they started digging.

Ayesha was intrigued by worms and insects she saw in the soil which she wasn't used to. She picked up a little lizard and stroked it.

She said, 'I think I'll keep it as a pet,' and put it in her pocket. She tried hard to find things to say to Noor.

She said, 'I believe your dad studies the hill tribes I've heard of.'

'Yes, and he does some archaeology too – digging up old bones and tools at the same time. He'd be interested in your people but hasn't time to follow it up.'

'Gosh, it's hard for me to think of someone being interested in us,' said Ayesha. 'Most people scorn us and shout nasty things at us in the street.'

'Why would they do that?'

'Because we're different, and don't really belong to the country. They see us as sponging on them. But we make a living from the sea and don't cause any trouble.'

'Goodness, is it so bad. The discrimination, I mean.'

'Yes, they call out rude things to me in the market. But I'm always well-behaved.'

'So they recognize you as belonging to your tribe when you look like any teenager.'

'They get to know us individually, by sight. I never talk back to them but just walk on.'

'I'll discuss this issue with my parents. They wouldn't approve of what's happening at all. I'd like to walk with you around the shops sometimes. I'll talk with people more about the class we go to and how nice you are.'

'Thanks, Noor. I think people are nicer to you than they are to me, and you are only a visitor to this country.'

'I'll always be your friend.'

Ayesha was nearly in tears. They had finished digging the whole vegie patch and now took the wheelbarrow to fetch the surplus soil. This was hard work too, digging it up and tossing it in the barrow. Several loads of that. Then raking it evenly over the top of the garden.

'Dad will be so pleased,' said Noor. 'Of course, I'll tell him you helped me.'

As they went into the house for lunch, Ayesha felt in her pocket for the lizard, but it had escaped. Noor introduced her mother.

She said, 'Mum is a nurse, but it's difficult for her to get work in a foreign country. She can speak English but not all patients can. She's called up for work at the hospital if they're short of nurses because of sickness.'

On another day, Noor said to Ayesha, 'My dad read about your people. They are special because their spleen is one and a half times bigger than the normal size. This has evolved over thousands of years. It helps them hold their breath longer under water, so they can dive deeper. Also, they can see better under water than normal people.'

'So, we are special people!'

'Yes. And they've survived for thousands of years.'

'Look how they are treated!'

'But you have to be educated to know and appreciate this. Also, Dad said some of these people are land dwellers and do farming. They have a horse-riding culture. I'll ask him if he can take us there sometime.'

When Ayesha went to the market some days later, a woman came up to her and said, 'I've heard you are attending a literacy class at the convent now.'

'Yes.'

'Well, congratulations! It's always good to better your life.'

A man nearby heard the conversation. He said, 'It's disgraceful that the Bajau are denied access to schools. I'm ashamed about it. Something should be done.'

'I agree,' said another man.

Another woman said, 'We've derided you in the past. I'm sorry.'

Goodness, thought Ayesha, they are being nice to me now. Noor must have gone around the market talking about me.

One evening when Ayesha got late and it was already quite dark, she passed the place where Jihad had stood with his motorbike, and someone grabbed her from behind around her neck. She cried out and felt she was being strangled. He – she thought it was a man – pulled her down to the ground. He was on top of her and she fought back with her fists, punching his chest as hard as she could, grunting with the effort of each blow. He was pulling down his trousers with one hand. She saw his face for a moment in the street light and shouted, 'Jihad! I know you, you're Jihad. Stop doing this.'

It took him by surprise and he hesitated. Maybe he did or didn't recognize her. Ayesha realized that it didn't matter, but by saying what she had said she'd humanized things. He couldn't go on with what he was doing. He drew back.

He said, 'I don't know you at all.' He sat up with a jerk. 'Get away from me, you slut.'

Ayesha scrambled to her feet and ran as fast as she could to the jetty where her canoe was.

Afterwards, she thought of the sexual thoughts he'd had and she felt violated, raped anyway. She was angry and cried. She didn't tell Mum about it.

Mum said, 'Don't come home so late. It's a bad time of day when it's getting dark.'

'I was talking with a man at the jetty.'

'Well, don't. Don't talk to strange men. They will take advantage of you.'

After the assault, Ayesha became afraid of walking to the jetty so late.

CHAPTER 6

Ayesha picked a bunch of flowers for Sister Rosa from a garden she was passing. There was no fence in the front.

'Where did you get the flowers?'

'They were growing in front of someone's house up to the sidewalk.'

'Don't you know the flowers belong to the person who lives in that garden?'

'But they are out in the open and I thought they wanted to share them.'

'Really, you have got the right idea, Ayesha, but you are stealing!'

To the class, Sister Rosa said, 'Now, what parables have you found that apply to your own lives?'

Noor said, 'The parable of the wise virgins who brought oil for their lamps and the foolish virgins who did not is like the story a friend told me about her wedding. The bridesmaids had posies of flowers to hold, but some of them forgot to bring them. There was no time for them to go and get them, and the bride was so cross that she stopped the ones with no posies from being bridesmaids. She needn't have, but they forgave her, apologized and were allowed to stay at the wedding.'

Concerning the parable of the unjust steward, Sunny said, 'My father, who is a business man, had a manager who he found was wasting his money, so he sacked him. The manager, desperate to get another job, asked people who he owed money to permit him to pay a lesser amount. So, then he'd wronged everyone.

'Jesus said, "No man can serve two masters, for he will hate the one and love the other. You cannot serve both God and money".'

Tomasin said, 'The story about the slaying of the powerful with a sword can be found in newspapers' reporting of crimes. When people have committed a murder, say, which was intended, they have often thought about it and rehearsed it in their minds a great deal, as opposed to the ones that occur on the spur of the moment.'

Ayesha said, 'I am like the woman in a parable, who is carrying a jar of flour. She dropped the jar and it broke, and the flour fell on the road. I let myself go without education when I knew it was something I should have. Eventually I sought it, and that was mainly because my young brother, Dido, died. I said to myself, I must not let my life slip away. My brother would have wanted me to have an education and I'll do it for his sake.'

To her surprise, all the class clapped. They said, 'Good on you, Ayesha!'

Hannah said, 'About the parable of the strong man, my father was always guarding his goods, but experienced a terrible loss when thieves got past his security and stole from his store. He became very angry, constantly saying what he'd do to the thieves. But the thieves were never apprehended.

'Eventually, my father had counselling with the whole

family. He learnt not to be so obsessed with property and to value the good things in life, like the rest of his family. He also learned not to guard his emotions so much, but to accept and feel more the beauty of many things, and the love of others. And he learned to share his thoughts and feelings more with his family, who could offer him comfort.'

Hannah looked sad as she spoke. She said she never thought she would tell such a personal story about someone in her family to other people, but it might help them.

Another student said she liked a beautiful parable related to the last because, like Hannah, she had Buddhist leanings. Reading from her notes, she said, 'There was a rich fool who owned ground which brought forth abundantly. He didn't have room to store his crops. He thought, I'll build a bigger barn. I will have many goods laid up for years, and will eat, drink and be merry. He ignored the poor and his neighbour.

'God said, "Foolish one, the things you have stored, whose will they be?"

'The parable means wealth cannot guarantee the future. The Day of Judgement may arrive sooner than you expect. I think it might be a day of judgement in this world, too.

'Jesus says, "Lay not up for yourself treasures on earth, where moth and rust do corrupt, and where thieves break through and steal, but lay up for yourselves treasures in Heaven. For where your treasure is, there will your heart be also".'

She said she liked that very much, even though she didn't believe in Heaven. People buy a lot of goods in the mistaken belief it will make them happy. But often it doesn't. If their basic needs are satisfied, they will be happier laying up treasures like helping, and giving joy and kindness to others.

Sister Rosa said, 'That is a good way of looking at it. You are right.'

At the Friday meeting, Ayesha said, 'Do you remember, Sunny, how you said a woman might come off worst in a relationship with a man?'

'Yes.'

'How would that be?'

'Women are more likely to be bullied in a relationship. I mean marriage. There might be physical or sexual violence from the man, even murder. Some men force women to have sex with them without their consent.'

'Jewish people don't do it,' said Gideon.

'I believe that's in exceptional cases,' added Jake.

'No, that's not true,' said Tomasin. 'I know about it. Societies cover it up and don't acknowledge it. It's too disturbing for people, some of whom are experiencing it themselves. Men won't admit to it. Women try to keep the family together.'

'There's nothing like that in my family,' said Ayesha. 'Except for the occasional tiff.'

Hannah said, 'I think women might come off worse in a family breakup because very often they have given up careers to bring up children and mightn't get enough financial support. Men do better and marry again, which is harder for the woman to do.'

'How do you know this?' said Ayesha.

'Oh, it's talked about at home. About our friends or other people.'

'My home life is a simple one,' said Ayesha. 'Everyone has to work so hard and must support one another as a necessity.'

That night, Princess Ayesha returned to tell more of her story.

She said: 'When I reached the age of eighteen, my father said it was time for him to find me someone to marry. I said I was too young and not interested in marriage. I wished to pursue cultural subjects like music and art more until I was older and fell in love. He would hear nothing of it. I would have to be sent away from home to another country where a high-ranking man could be found who was an equal of the king. So, I would not even know the man I was to marry. I would be separated from my parents.'

'I feel sorry for you,' said Ayesha. 'You had to bear all this so young.'

'I begged my father not to send me away, but he would not listen. My mother cried at the thought of it, but she could do nothing. I realized I had no power or control over my life, and I was humiliated.'

'You could have run away from home.'

'That was unthinkable to me as the person I was then. After a while, my father told me he had found a good husband for me and I would be provided with everything a princess would want or need. This was what a person of

my standing was expected to do, and I should be grateful for my privileges. He next made arrangements for me to be taken to my future husband in a neighbouring country. I see you are nodding off and will speak again another time.'

Ayesha found out about a drop-in centre where she could get a free lunch. After many visits to it, she often saw, on the way, an old woman who scavenged for food in trash bins.

'You can have a free meal at the newly opened canteen,' she said. 'It's a drop-in centre for those who don't have food, a home, a job. Come with me and I'll show you where it is.'

The woman said, 'I'll feel ashamed.'

'No one will shame you. All people who go there are in the same boat.'

The woman said, 'Oh, all right,' in a resigned way, and went along with Ayesha.

When they entered the centre, there was a receptionist who asked the woman for her first name only. 'If you sit at the table over there, someone will bring you a plate of food.'

Ayesha sat with the woman so she wouldn't feel isolated. They were the only ones at the table as it wasn't yet lunchtime. A volunteer appeared shortly with a sandwich and a glass of milk. The old lady ate and drank readily.

Ayesha said, 'In this centre, you can have a bed for the night if you need it, or a chair to sit in, or a nice hot shower. They'll give you a change of second-hand clothes.'

'They will ask me awkward questions about my life.'

'No, they won't. They'll try to find out if you need a nurse or doctor. There is a clinic you can go to. You can always find company here if you feel lonely.'

Ayesha soon volunteered to help serve at the tables in return for the free lunch. She did a lot of housework at the centre; sweeping, dusting and wiping things clean. It was a novelty for her as she never did it at home. Mum did it.

Bringing plates of food for people, she met an Irish university student working on a six-month visa. He wasn't paid for work he did at the centre, which was mostly washing up, but he had a free bed and meals.

'Are you a student from abroad?' he asked her.

'No, I live locally and am a literacy student at the convent.'

Gradually, Ayesha told him about her background and how she had never been to school before her recent classes. He was shocked.

'This doesn't occur anywhere else in the world, to my knowledge.'

'I'm making up for it the best I can. I've come to the drop-in centre to try to do something good in the world. My teacher, Sister Rosa, teaches us to read, and write about, the parables of Jesus.'

Ayesha thought she was getting too much attention from a down-and-out man at the centre.

The next time Ayesha saw Jihad near the jetty, he looked

cool and collected as a cucumber.

She confronted him. 'Hello, Jihad.'

He said 'Hello' and stared blankly at her. Deliberately, as if she were just a passer-by.

'You recall we met, of course.'

He shrugged.

Ayesha went on, 'I will do what Christians do and turn the other cheek. It means I will be your friend even though you treated me badly and might continue to do so.'

Jihad looked embarrassed.

'If you pay a person back, they do the same and it goes on and on. My people don't believe in payback. Tell me, why is your nickname Jihad?'

'I was too aggressive to other kids.'

'Oh. I see you are never doing much. Would you like to come to the literacy class I attend? It would improve your reading and writing.'

'I already went to school.'

'Why did you leave early?' She was sure he hadn't finished school. He looked too young. Younger than her.

'It was boring.'

'Well, think about the classes. They are free. Sister Rosa doesn't treat students like children, but like adults. You could leave if you don't like it. Would you think of coming?'

'I already tried the classes because my mother wanted me to, but I couldn't stand the religion. Sister Rosa gave me the creeps. I told the students about the Muslim separatists – how they want a separate country.'

'Oh.' Ayesha started to walk away.

Raising his voice, Jihad said, 'I wasn't going to have you but was overcome by sexual desires.'

Ayesha turned and said, 'You should learn to control your aggressive urges. They might be caused by testosterone, a hormone boys have, but that's not an excuse. You are held responsible for your actions by law, even if you are not truly able to exercise responsibility.'

Afterwards, Ayesha realized he probably made that up about going to the literacy class.

CHAPTER 7

When Ayesha was paddling to the shore, a water spout popped up to one side of her. Then another just behind. They were columns of air, dragging up water and swirling it round. She imagined one of them picking her up and plopping her down somewhere else. It was a fun idea. But it didn't happen today. At the jetty, Odin was laughing.

'I saw you surrounded by waterspouts and was waiting for one to tip you into the water!'

Sister Rosa told the students to take a story from one of the parables and see if they could find something similar in real life. They might like to work in pairs. Ayesha and Gideon chose each other and got together to discuss what they might do. They thought they would find a situation at the dockyards which resembled the parable of the labourers in the vineyard.

In this parable, a householder hired labourers to work in his vineyard early in the morning. He hired more as the day progressed. But at the end of the day, he paid them all the same amount. When some disagreed, he said, 'You agreed with me about the daily wage. I can do what I like with my money.'

Jesus said, 'The last shall be first, and the first last, for many may be called, but few chosen.'

Ayesha and Gideon fixed on a day and, after the market, Ayesha went to Gideon's house. Together, they walked down to the docks. It was still early but very busy. Nearer to the shore, a crane was loading huge boxes of goods onto a cargo ship.

They found a group of casual workers in a rough line outside the office door of a shipping company. The workers went there every morning to pick up whatever jobs they could. The men were trying to attract the attention of a particular man who came in and out of the door to carry out business. He was the one who would hire them if they were needed.

Ayesha and Gideon decided to speak to someone inside the office first, to find out whether the men looking for work were paid the same for the whole day regardless of what time they started work. When they entered the office and approached the official, he treated them in a brusque manner.

'I'm too busy, as you can see, to be interviewed by students for their assignments. You should ask the men outside, who have plenty of time on their hands.'

Gideon and Ayesha went back outside and explained their purpose to the men, who crowded around to hear. The men said they were paid by the hour from the time they were hired. The situation we were describing didn't exist but, if it did, they thought each person should be paid for the period of time they were hired.

'But supposing you were usually paid for the whole day regardless of when you arrived,' said Gideon.

'Yes, that is okay, but paying each person only for the

time they work is fairest. If you paid all of us for the same amount of time, we would be disgruntled,' said one man. The others agreed.

When they were walking back to town, Ayesha said, 'They didn't agree with Jesus.'

'I think the labourers Jesus was talking about were much poorer and more dependent than those on the docks, who might have a union looking after their interests.'

On another day, Gideon and Ayesha thought they would find a situation like that of the parable of the hidden treasure if they went to a farm. The kingdom of Heaven was like a treasure hidden in a field, which a man discovered. In his joy, he went out and sold all that he had to buy the field. The hidden nature of the treasure showed that the kingdom of Heaven was not yet revealed to all. To possess Heavenly riches, one must be willing to give up the world to buy it.

So Gideon borrowed his father's car and they went for a day trip into the hill country at the back of the town, where there were small farms which grew vegetables and had fruit orchards. At some places, you could buy fruit and vegetables directly from the farmer. They arrived at one which had a notice on the gate saying there were tomatoes for sale, and drove in.

The farmer said, 'You can pick the tomatoes you want yourselves,' and gave them a basket. They went to pick the tomatoes.

While Gideon was paying for the tomatoes, Ayesha said to the farmer, 'Do you realize that your harvest is ultimately not of your work, nor of nature, but of God, and do you treasure what God has given?'

'I do, if you put it that way, but I think it's more of nature. Sometimes nature gives, and sometimes it takes away. I do believe in God and I do treasure what he has given in all respects. My life and that of my family, and the whole world.'

'And do you realize your farm belongs to God and you are the caretaker?'

'I do.'

Gideon and Ayesha wrote a report of their projects to read to the class. Ayesha read it aloud, and then said, 'I can include a conversation we've written about having lunch with Gideon afterwards. Do you want to hear it?'

'Yes, yes,' everyone said.

'We found a nice spot to have a picnic by a river. We had brought sandwiches.

'I said, "Gideon, what do you treasure in life?"

"My family."

"Me too. Without them, I wouldn't be able to achieve anything, having little education."

"Yes, I value my education, such as it is."

"We won't give up on education then, will we."

"Not for anything. It's what we have to do to get anywhere."

"We're so lucky to have food and somewhere to sleep. I see the life of poor people every day in town."

"I must go to university one day so I can train for a proper job."

"I don't think I'll be able to do that – no money."

"Why not? You can at least apply for a scholarship."

"People will discriminate against me for a job, or anything, because I'm a Bajau."

"You really think that."

"I do."'

Ayesha had finished and looked up. There was moment of silence when the students thought about what she'd said.

'You should go to university,' said Tomasin. 'You are an intelligent person. It's no drawback to lack schooling. You can sit a test.'

'It's ridiculous for me to think of going to university. I know almost nothing but the parables of Jesus.'

Hannah said, 'They won't discriminate against you at university level.'

'But it's hard for me to think that. I'm always apprehensive.'

'You should treasure yourself more – but I know it's easy to say,' said Noor. 'You are like the treasure in the field. God has given you this treasure. If you make use of it for good, people will recognize it.'

'I hope to do good for my people,' said Ayesha. I wonder if Gideon would like me, she thought.

The Princess Ayesha came back to speak that night. She said, 'On the appointed day of my leaving home, the royal guards were ordered to escort me to the ruler of the neighbouring country who would marry me. I would be able to see my family again, as they would be invited to the wedding. I would travel in a carriage drawn by horses, with the guards riding on horseback beside it. I cried and cried as I said goodbye. My mother cried a great deal too. She knew I didn't want to go, but she had no power to do anything about it.

'When we reached the border of our own country, we had to cross a wide river at a point where it was near the sea. A great storm suddenly swept in when we were halfway across the river, and the tide rose high even there. Waves were crashing over the carriage and it toppled over. I would have drowned had not a guardsman saved me. Clasping me to his side, he used all his strength to swim until we reached dry land on the farther bank, in a deserted part of the foreign country. He told me to hold onto a tree trunk, and the next minute he was carried away by a wave.'

'That must have been terrible,' said Ayesha.

'Yes. I clung to the trunk with all my might and prayed to God,' said the princess. 'I think many of the guards drowned. Any still alive would have returned to the castle believing I had died.'

Ayesha had escaped into sleep.

She found Jihad the next day standing beside his motorbike, as usual, on the side of the road and near the jetty, watching people go by. He told her he had been accosted by a young man, who said, 'You look as if you don't have anything to do.'

Jihad had said, 'I don't have a job now. I might pick one up, standing here. Deliveries.'

'What's your name?'

'Jihad.'

'That's a very distinctive name. You must be

Muslim.'

'Yes.'

'I work with a Muslim group who make good money. You might like to join us.'

'What do you do?'

'You will learn if you join us.'

'How do I join?'

'Come to a meeting of our group and find out.'

Jihad had said he would come to the meeting, and the man told him when and where it was. Here, Jihad learnt that they kidnapped wealthy people or tourists and held them hostage in a jungle hideout until they paid a ransom to be freed. Jihad became their apprentice.

'Don't you think that is immoral?' said Ayesha.

'I can't say,' said Jihad sheepishly. 'They are sick of the government always being biased against Muslims and want a separate Islamic state or country of their own. They worked on me to join them.'

'I can't believe it. What did you have to do as an apprentice?'

Jihad said, 'I went with another man by motorcycle to do a kidnapping, while a third man parked a car in a nearby street. I and the second man drove up on either side of a car driven by a man. The other kidnapper was on the driver's side, and he drew his gun and pointed it at the driver. The driver now stopped on the side of the road, put his hands up and handed over his phone and wallet. However, the gunman, holding a gun to the driver's head, made him get out of the car, blindfolded him, tied his hands and, with my help, forced him into the car parked nearby. We all drove back to a separatists' hideout.'

'What did they do then?'

'He had to pay a larger sum of money than was in his wallet to get back his freedom.'

Ayesha had a disgusted expression on her face.

Jihad said, 'There are much worse people in the world. You're lucky you found me.'

'Are there any of these Muslims who don't do kidnapping?' said Ayesha. 'I would be interested to know more about them. Do you know of someone who would be willing to talk with me about it?'

Jihad said he would find out. The next time he saw her, he said that Omar, in a different group, would be happy to talk with her.

'He will come to this spot at this time to see you.'

CHAPTER 8

Ayesha was paddling to the shore, and was almost there, when she heard the cries of a woman who had got out of her depth in the ocean. She paddled closer to the woman and tried to pull her up into the canoe, which was loaded with fish. The canoe tipped to one side and it seemed as though all would fall into the water. She jumped into the water to steady the canoe and told the woman to drag herself into it. The woman managed to clamber in, and Ayesha followed.

'What were you doing in the ocean?' she said.

'I was looking for shellfish – you can find some just close to the shore. The current pulled me out deeper.'

Ayesha dropped her off at the jetty. I've often done this, she thought. Her clothes were all wet – she had to leave them to dry out on her.

When she went to have lunch at the drop-in centre, a young man she had seen there before sat down opposite her at the table.

He said, 'What is your name?'

'Ayesha. What is yours?'

'Chris.'

He had a sort of faded, nondescript appearance, with light brown hair, eyes and skin, and worn clothing. He had strong muscles in his arms.

He said, 'I see you come here most days for lunch.'

'Yes. I've said hello to you. As I don't have any money to spare, I sometimes serve at the tables too. I sell fish my father catches at the market and use the money to buy other foods we need.'

'I do odd jobs,' said Chris. 'I'm not working today. Sometimes, I don't have work.'

Ayesha saw he was brushing specks of dirt off his old, worn shirt. He had dirty fingernails.

'I've been in hospital with cancer,' said Chris, 'but I'm better now.'

'You must take your time to rest and recover.'

'Yes, people are always saying that.'

After lunch, Chris asked Ayesha if she would walk with him a little. She explained how she was going to literacy classes, so he accompanied her to the convent. He was nice, pleasant to talk with. She had a better impression of him now. She recalled that Jesus had said, 'Do not judge by appearances, but with right judgement.'

Chris said, 'I saw you once at the docks. You were there with another man. Is he your boyfriend?'

'Oh no, he is a student in my class. We were doing a project together.'

She wasn't going to mention any personal relation with Gideon that she thought she might have.

Sister Rosa had told the students to go out and find people who needed help and try to help them. This was what good Christians would do.

'You are to write a report on your good deeds, but I

don't mind if you tell it like a story or make it amusing, but you must tell the truth.'

Sunny read from his report, 'I gave away presents to the street children, with plenty of food. These children are from very poor families. Some are orphans, but there is no space left in orphanages for them. They don't go to school but try to sell things or do jobs on the street.

'I said to a boy, "How do you manage to sell things or do jobs?'

'The boy said, "Well, I stop cars to ask people if they will buy things or give me a job. Or I ask someone in the street."

"Do you ever sleep in a bed in a house?"

"Sometimes I get into a special children's shelter, but often I miss out because they don't have enough beds."

'So, at night, I thought, these children have to sleep on the ground in a train station, or in a doorway, or on a park bench. They might be bashed by a thief, who steals their money.

'I went to the children's shelter to see how things were. I told them I was a Buddhist because I knew the shelter was run by Buddhists. They said it was true they don't have enough beds, through lack of funds.

'I said, "If people truly believe in Buddhism, they would donate their money like Buddha gave away his wealth to the poor. Buddhists want to live in a world where there is justice, friendship and peace".'

'Can you do anything to help these children?' said Sister Rosa.

'I'll try.'

Gideon read, 'I heard from my father of a person who needed assistance with his tax return and other things.

"I am not a tax consultant," I said.

"No," said Dad, "but I believe it is quite lowbrow work. You'll be able to help."

"So I assisted the elderly man fill in his tax form and pay some bills. He asked me to come back to do more paperwork, and I did. He was grateful for it.'

Jake read his report of doing good, 'I helped a man who was lying in the gutter. He seemed to be drunk. His breath smelled of alcohol. People wouldn't help him, like something Tomasin said, they wouldn't want to associate in public with someone so disreputable. But I was becoming addicted to alcohol myself, once.'

'When you were only a school kid?' said a student.

'Yes. I gave a false age at the liquor store, paid for the bottle with my pocket money and hid it in my room.

'Anyway, I roused the man from his stupor, in which he was mumbling to himself. I helped him to his feet, seeing, at the same moment, that he had vomited and had vomit on his mouth. I took a tissue in my pocket and wiped his mouth. I had to support the man, who was swaying about. I managed to get him to walk some stumbling steps.

'"Where do you live?" I asked.

'I couldn't understand what the man replied but he seemed to know where he was going. So I escorted him home in this fashion and saw that he got into bed. I found a glass in the bathroom and filled it with water. I tried to make him drink, but the water mostly dribbled down his chin. I left the water beside his bed.'

Noor presented her report of being a do-gooder, 'I helped an old woman to cross the road in a heavy downpour, when the road was flooded from lack of proper drainage. I supported her arm and we both waded through water up to our knees in the storm surge. The woman was shaking and could barely move her legs against the downhill force of the current. When we reached the other side, the old lady thanked me profusely for my assistance.

"'The rain came so suddenly," she said. "I wouldn't have crossed the road in the first place if I had known what would happen!"'

Hannah read her report, 'I gave up my seat on the bus to a heavily pregnant woman. When she got off at her stop, I followed her and said I would accompany her home carrying her bags. She was pleased. At the door, she invited me in for coffee, which I accepted. I asked her if she would like help with housework as I would be glad to do it. I told her more about my life, and that the students were asked to practise Christianity in their lives. She was impressed, and we cleaned her house together.'

Tomasin read, 'I rushed halfway across the road to grab a small boy before he was hit by a car. The boy cried when I picked him up so suddenly. I ran back to the pavement with him. The parents had noticed their child had got away by now and came straight up to take him from me. He bawled as soon as he saw them. They thanked me, and I left at once. It's funny that the kid cried more when he saw his parents.'

Ayesha told her story of rescuing the woman from the sea. She wasn't expected to write a report on her own.

After the reports had been read, Sister Rosa said they should follow up their good deeds by seeing if they could do more for the person they'd helped.

What happened to Princess Ayesha after she survived the storm? wondered Ayesha.

The princess continued her story: 'I was freezing cold and nearly letting go of the tree trunk, but a fisherman came to my aid. He took me to his hut for shelter. I told him I was on my way to marry the ruler of his country, but he couldn't understand my language. He and his wife proved to be very kind people and they more or less adopted me as their daughter. I felt so useless, being unable to do almost anything for myself let alone others. For the first time, I felt humble in my life. I was in no rush to try and meet up with a man I didn't want to marry, but I supposed someone would find where I was eventually. And they did – a stranger.'

'You must have found it a very different life.'

'Yes, and difficult because I knew nothing about what the fisher folk had to do to make their living and I was not used to hard physical work. I later learned that it was thought I had drowned with the guardsmen. The people of my father's kingdom had been ordered to search for me, but they had no success. As a result, some of them gradually became sea-faring people for fear of the wrath of the king. But that was far in the future.'

'So that was how our culture began?' said Ayesha.

'Yes, and though fishers of the sea, they still practise agricultural rituals like the first rice harvest, which show

their origin. You might have heard that the boy who founded our tribe was sent by the king to search for the princess. This is wrong. Why would a child be sent to look for her? But my son, who was about eighteen by then, did become their leader. The king didn't know of his existence and passed on the wrong story.'

Ayesha murmured something, but she didn't hear any reply to it because she had been lulled into sleep.

When Ayesha next came to the place near the jetty where Jihad usually stood, another man was waiting there. She stopped walking and looked at him.

He said, 'I'm Omar. Are you Ayesha?'

'I am.'

'Jihad told me about you. He said you are a Bajau and are interested in my group.'

'Yes, my people are similar to yours in their beliefs. I want to know more about your movement to get a separate Muslim state.'

'The government sold our traditional lands to non-Muslims in the past and we are lobbying to get them back. Your people are Muslim, similar to ours, like cousins, and could join us as equal citizens of our state, when we get it.'

'So we would have citizenship?'

'Yes, and education. But I want to warn you, the jihadists are a different mob. They are not just traditional Muslims, but some are modern young men from anywhere in the world, with a grouch against society, who have aligned themselves with Islamic ideas interpreted in an extreme form. Their jihad is a daily fight against the enemies of Islam, which they impose by force. Some of them go in for torture and cutting off people's limbs or heads.'

'Are they the ones who kidnap people for a ransom?'

'Yes. We only use peaceful means. We Muslims are hospitable people, and we will have to accept the jihadists being in our separate state and try to live with them as a democratic society. But if they are prevented from getting away with their horrible acts, many may just go to another part of the world to stir up trouble.'

'But what about the radical ones that don't leave? They believe the highest deed is jihad – above fasting and prayer. It is a noble life to die as a martyr.'

'They are a small group. Some have been indoctrinated in terrorism in special schools for Muslim boys in our own country, which is against the law. It is a fault that lies within our society.'

CHAPTER 9

When Ayesha and Gideon first kissed, they were standing under a dim lamp in the street. Gideon suddenly turned towards her and she didn't anticipate it. He put his arms around her, pulling her towards him. She raised her face to look at his eyes. He bent his face down and kissed her straight on the mouth and she put her arms around his waist. Overcome with intense feelings of love, she whispered 'I love you'. He said 'I love you' back.

They stayed like that for a long time, motionless. It seemed they would never part, and they had a complete love affair lasting a lifetime in those moments. Eventually, they moved away; neither wanted to. As Ayesha came out of her enchantment, self-conscious, she imagined other people looking at them – what did they think? Did they think it was shameful lust or a young man and woman in love?

Ayesha had been attracted to Gideon immediately, but they had difficulty talking with each other. Ayesha felt awkward. Gideon seemed physically and personality-wise strong and confident, but not with women. He wasn't practised in talking with girls. He was purposeful, a bit controlling and often thought he was right, she thought.

Gideon invited Ayesha to his house for dinner. He met her at the jetty and took her to his home. His father, the rabbi, greeted them at the door and showed them into the lounge room.

'My wife is just finishing the cooking. Could I get you a fruit juice?' he said to Ayesha.

'Yes, thanks.' She felt shy. What do you say to a rabbi? But Gideon had told her to just treat his father like any other person.

After they exchanged a few pleasantries, Gideon's mother came in and said dinner was ready, and to please come to the table.

'Gideon and I are enjoying our English class,' said Ayesha.

'Ayesha could hardly read or write and has made great progress,' said Gideon.

'Would you think of going to university?' said the rabbi.

'What me?' said Ayesha. 'I haven't contemplated it. I'm not at that level.'

'Gideon is planning to take science. He's good at literature too.'

'We read something about your people,' said Gideon's mother, Ruth. She had asked Ayesha to use her first name.

'We are a proud people,' Ayesha said.

'I should think so, with the type of life you have.'

Gideon said he thought Ayesha was a lovely person. She hid her light under a bushel.

'Let your light shine in the world, Ayesha,' said the rabbi.

Gideon's parents gave her to understand they

expected Gideon to marry someone Jewish.

The students decided to collect old clothes and take them to the poor. They did this as a group in their spare time, door-knocking to collect the clothes and taking them around a known poorer district. They could write up what they did in reports they read to their class.

They organized themselves into pairs to go around together. Ayesha and Noor paired off. They walked to a rich part of the town. They only had a trolley they took from a supermarket to push the clothes in.

At the first house, a maid answered the door. They told her what they were doing.

The maid said, 'Wait here. I will ask my lady if she has some old clothes put aside for throwing away.'

'Tell her we are older students from the convent,' said Noor.

When the maid returned, she said, 'You may come in.'

She showed them into the lounge room. After a while, the lady of the house appeared.

She said, 'I've been looking to see what I've got for you to take.'

'Thank you,' said Ayesha. 'We're doing a project with Sister Rosa about helping others and doing good deeds.'

'Well, I certainly support you in that,' said the lady.

They went with her to her bedroom, where she had already put some clothes in plastic bags. They waited while she found more things. Then they carried several bundles to the trolley.

After Ayesha and Noor had done the same work in several houses, their trolley was full. They hadn't worked out how to continue. It would be a long walk to the poor part of town.

They took a short cut through a park. Some young children were playing a ball game and one threw the ball into the trolley by mistake. Ayesha threw it back.

A child said, 'You are spoiling our game.' They were glad to get clear of the children.

Later, as they approached the poor district, they were accosted by some teenage boys.

They said, 'Are you stealing the clothes? Here, let us get them!'

Ayesha and Noor had to fight them off, saying that they were women's second-hand clothes they would be giving to the boys' mums. The boys lost interest.

It looked like being a long day's work for Ayesha and Noor. Exhausted, they happened to see Jake and Tomasin, who were driving a car, and the four of them joined forces to get through a great deal more of their enterprise that day.

When they were in a district, they were stopped by a man who said, 'You are infidels.'

They all said, 'We are not.'

'You are students at the convent. They are Christian. We're keeping an eye on you.'

'Who's "we"? We're going there for literacy classes.'

'Really? We'll see about that. It's not necessary for women to read and write.'

'Yes, it is,' said Tomasin, 'especially so, hearing from people like you.'

Ayesha thought, Jihad must have said something about us. He might live near here. He knows these people. He would talk about things.

That night, Princess Ayesha went on: 'My story spread to many people because I was a princess. A rumour went around that I had not died, and a sultan of another country was one of those who heard it. As he wished to marry a princess, he came looking for me around the location of the river where I had disappeared. On the way to it, by sea, he was actually attacked by the forces of the very man I was supposed to marry. Driving the troops off, the sultan headed for the mouth of the river where there was calm water for making a landing. Here it was that he saw the fisherman's boat, and the cottage where I lived. It was in a remote part of the country, cut off by high rocks but accessible by sea. The fisherman was used to taking his catch to market in a town farther up the river.

'The fisherman had gradually understood what happened to me. When the stranger came enquiring about a girl who might have survived an accident in the river, the fisherman managed to convey to him that the girl was me, and he had adopted me. He called me over from where I was working, and I found I could speak a common language with the stranger. I explained how I'd come from the neighbouring country and was left abandoned on the bank of the river, after I had almost drowned following a tidal surge in a storm. My escort had either drowned or returned to the king.'

'Would he believe you were a princess?' said Ayesha.

'He could still see I was wearing fine clothes, though they were now shabby from wear and work. I said, in my cultured manner, that I was a princess and had been on my way to marry a ruler whom I didn't wish to marry. If I returned to my family, I would not be welcome. The stranger recognized this story was entirely true. He told me he was a sultan of another country. After a few days thinking about everything on his ship, the sultan returned to the fisherman's hovel with a proposition.

'Are you still listening to me, Ayesha? This is important.' But hearing no reply, the princess stopped speaking.

At their weekly meeting, some students came up with the idea of holding a fair or fete at the showgrounds. Different religious and community groups could present their cultures in activities and speeches. It would be held on the day of a special Bajau celebration of their culture, if they were willing, show-casing their dancing, singing and crafts. There would be stalls selling anything, and amusements. The students were all enthusiastic to do it.

Sister Rosa had asked the members of the class to describe the religion they belonged to, or their lack of religion. Some of these talks could be presented at the fair, instead of in class.

'I will give my talk on Jinn at the fair as part of the Bajau presentation,' said Ayesha.

'The Buddhists monks could do their chanting, so I'll do my talk about Buddhism then,' said Hannah.

'I won't,' said Gideon, 'because people would be

bored by Judaism, which they've either never heard of or they know all they want about Jews.'

'I won't either,' said Noor, 'because people always get hot around the collar about Islam, and bring up all sorts of questions and criticisms, and the audience will get angry with one another about it, and nothing will be resolved. I'll be happy to have a discussion with fellow students.'

When Ayesha saw Jihad again, he told her more about the separatist group he had joined. She asked if she could go with him to a meeting of the group, as she wanted to find out what they were doing, for herself. So Jihad arranged for her to meet him at the same place near the jetty to go to the meeting with him.

As they arrived, the men at the door welcomed her. They all had dark facial hair and beards but otherwise their appearance was like anyone else. Ayesha looked around the group to see if women were present, but they weren't.

She said, 'Where are the women?'

A man said, 'They are at home taking care of children and doing household tasks.'

While they were waiting for the speaker to address the group, Ayesha said to Jihad, 'Where did you meet such people?'

'They talked to me in the street, like you. They were particularly interested in my nickname, as I told you, which means "holy war". Their main belief is that a holy war is needed.'

The audience now clustered together. The eyes of the men seemed to flash with anger. Ayesha thought, was it the anger of righteous indignation?

The leader of the group spoke up. 'We are here with God's blessing to advocate and advance our cause against the infidel. Our aim is to fight until we have an Islamic state no longer occupied or dominated by non-Muslims. We will no longer bow down and obey them. We will attack with guns and bombs until their system collapses. We will destroy their books, statues and churches. We have been ripped off and will restore our territory and rights.'

'Hear, hear!' the crowd cheered.

'If one of you turns against us, we will execute him. Let that be a warning,' the leader continued. 'We do not fear being martyrs. We resist with our blood. We will go straight to Heaven.'

After the meeting, Ayesha felt fearful of these people. She hoped she would never again have anything to do with them. They were false prophets.

CHAPTER 10

Sister Rosa had said the students could look up information on the Internet about their religion and write notes to bring to class. Several students told her that they knew about their religion from their parents, but Sister Rosa insisted what they would discover was that their parents didn't know everything about it.

Gideon said to everyone, 'I belong to the religion of Judaism, which is in a book called the Torah. It contains the laws and commandments that God revealed to Moses on Mount Sinai. I regard these as guidelines for living my life, but my father is stricter and thinks of them as law. We should only love and worship one god and love one another.

'I have a story to tell. I asked some people in Israel, "How can we stop the Palestinians and Israelis fighting each other?"

'A woman who was a teacher said, "Some of us believe we might unite people if they have a love of nature. Birds don't have boundaries between them, so we are teaching people to be like a bird."

'I said, "I believe birds do have boundaries. Climate change might change their boundaries so that they fight and destroy one another".'

Varsha had only just joined the class. She said her

family came from India and her father worked as an engineer. She had a brother who was younger. Her mother was an English teacher and could get work in relief teaching for teachers who were sick. She, herself, spoke good English, but had joined the class to improve it and to meet new people.

She said, 'My religion is Hinduism. It is *dharma* or a way of life, which emphasizes authority and eternal truths, but also questions authority. There are eternal duties like honesty and not harming others. God is *Brahman.* We believe in the soul. You've probably heard of *karma:* your actions and intentions have consequences which may be for good or do harm, and this spreads out to many people.'

A new student said, 'I want to speak about the Baha'i faith. This teaches that religious truth is manifested and revealed by the founders of all world religions. The guardian of the Baha'i faith, at their Universal House of Justice, is guided by the book of laws of the founder, Baha'u'llah, to exert a positive influence on the welfare of humans and all nature, and promote education, religion, equality, peace and global prosperity. The human progresses spiritually by serving others and has eternal life.'

'That sounds very commendable,' said Sister Rosa. 'Are you a member of the Baha'i faith?'

'I am not because I've only just heard of it, but I admire and respect what they believe in. The world would be a better place if we tried to achieve their ideals. They are so inclusive.'

Noor said, 'I know many of you will have questions

about Islam. Islam has six main beliefs: Allah is the one and only God; the angels, holy books, the prophets, and the day of judgement. Jesus is one of the six prophets. The main holy book is the Quran. Allah knows everything in the past, present and future, but humans have free will. Allah created and rules everything. Religion requires obedience to Allah's will. Allah has no form or gender and can't be seen.

'There are five obligatory acts of worship called the Five Pillars: the profession of faith "There is no god but God, and Muhammad is the Messenger of God" (Muhammad's life is the "trodden path"); prayer five times a day and to memorize and recite the Quran; to give money to the poor; to fast at Ramadan; and to make a pilgrimage to Mecca at least once in your life.'

'How are we to take in all these details and make something of it?' said Ayesha. 'It's like a list of orders.'

'You're right. I didn't even know most of it until I read it on the Internet. I'll just finish it briefly. Sharia law governs all: a man is allowed up to four wives; circumcision is mandatory; there are diet restrictions; women's coverings represent modesty; and there are social welfare values. In Heaven, there will be an ecstatic awareness of God. *Phew!*'

Tomasin, who had not spoken much in the class, said she had written down some comparisons between Christianity and Islam. 'In Christianity, salvation is by Grace through faith in Christ; in Islam, it is through good works, so that personal righteousness outweighs personal sin. Christians and Muslims believe in one God, creator of everything that exists, but disagree on the nature of God and what he expects from humans. Muslims regard God as merciful and benevolent but don't necessarily think of God as loving. Christians believe, because of love, God sent his son to atone for sin. Christians are to love God, their neighbour, and even their enemies.'

Tomasin pointed out that Islam and Judaism have no clergy but have scholars and judges. Both these religions have diet restrictions like not eating pork.

'Any questions?' said Sister Rosa. A host of hands went up. She pointed to Hannah.

'I object to the unequal treatment of women in Islam, such as in divorce laws and men being allowed to have four wives.'

Noor said, 'The Quran says men and women have equal rights to life, education, property and free choice. All I can say about polygamy is that there is nothing about it in the Quran. I, and other Muslims, believe that the divorce laws should be equal between the sexes as in modern societies. In many Muslim countries, change is happening.'

'So humans only have free will to fulfil Allah's will,' said Jake sarcastically. No one else commented.

'Muslims really mean that Allah is different from the God of Christianity, don't they,' said Sunny.

'That's true,' said Noor, 'but it isn't specifically stated in the texts. In Christianity, God is a god of love above all else.'

'Likewise, God of the Old Testament is different from God of the New Testament,' said Tomasin.

'I am horrified about the punishments handed out to sinners in some countries who break Islamic law, like stoning to death, or cutting off body parts that were sinned with,' said Gideon.

'I don't support these things,' said Noor. 'Many people in the world speak out against them. They are ancient punishments but are in the Quran.'

'I don't believe in people going straight to Heaven if they die fighting in a holy war,' said Ayesha. 'The war might be unjustified.'

'I agree,' said some members of the class.

'You are all attacking Islam too much,' said Noor.

'You're a good sport, Noor, and courageous,' said Sister Rosa.

'What about the Roman Catholic priests who abuse children,' Noor pointed out, not flinching.

'We don't approve of those either,' said Jake.

'I know about these things,' said Sister Rosa, but added nothing more on the subject. 'To say something neutral, the Islamic belief in not representing God in pictures or sculptures is different to Christian practice.'

'It's in the Old Testament,' said Gideon, 'not to make graven images of sacred objects.'

Jake said, 'All religions are authoritarian by nature.'

'Protestantism is not,' said Tomasin.

'Yes it is, if you have to believe in God.'

'Buddhism is not authoritarian,' said Sunny.

'Neither is Jinn,' said Ayesha. 'But what about the jihadists who want a separate state?'

'They are not true Muslims,' said Noor.

'My goodness, we *have* had a long discussion!' said Sister Rosa. 'It's time to go home. The talks about Jinn and Buddhism have been deferred to the fete and fair being planned.'

Sunny said, 'Remember to finalize all your arrangements for the fete. It's in only two weeks.'

'You should all attend,' said Ayesha. 'It's terribly important to me.'

At the jetty, a man came up to her and said, 'You Bajau don't pay taxes and rates like everyone else.'

She didn't answer and walked straight to the canoe. That's a new one, she thought. As if I were responsible for such a matter! I suppose it's because we're stateless and have no access to services. When will we be treated as equals?

In the night, Princess Ayesha told her what the sultan proposed: 'He said he would like to buy me from the fisherman and offered him a sum of money that he couldn't refuse. He would be able to have a fine house in town and a much better boat. When I remonstrated, no one paid any attention because what else could I do but accept it.'

'Of course,' said Ayesha, 'the fisherman accepted the offer and was obliged to give you to the sultan, who could have forced you to go with him. You were now his possession.'

'The sultan said he had fallen in love with me and wanted to marry me. He was a Muslim like me. He was a nice man. I realized I would prefer to marry him than to be returned to my family, if he allowed it, for then I would

only be dispatched again to the previous suitor.'

'Better the devil you know!' said Ayesha.

'You could say that. I had become much humbler in my attitude to life by this time. I was grateful that I would not have to live in poverty and, knowing what it was like, glad that the fisherman and his wife would enjoy their wealth. They deserved it. It was a reward for having almost certainly saved my life.'

CHAPTER 11

Ayesha saw clouds of birds in the sky. Sometimes, that happens, she thought. Or clouds of insects. Silvery sky streaked with pink; a thunderhead gathering. They were signs that bad weather was on the way. Gideon had told her there were more storms now because of climate change.

She said to Ma, 'I think a cyclone is coming, and I heard it from Sister Rosa too. You'll have to stock up on fish.'

Ma and Dad passed the message to other households in their group. They wouldn't dive for fish if it rained, because visibility would be reduced owing to less light and more mud and sediment in the water. Access to and exit from the house would be difficult, and even impossible.

When the cyclone hit, the whole house shuddered and strained in the force of the wind, creaking and groaning. They could only just see the storm pummelling the coastline. They had withstood these cyclones before. Dad had built the house so strongly that it had never collapsed or blown away. The roof had stayed on.

Dad said, 'The spirits are angry.'

Ayesha told her class later, 'Waves started to penetrate the floor through the cracks between the floor boards. Everything was getting wet. The rain made a clapping sound. Then there was a terrific noise like a plane flying over. The house leaned in one direction, but the doors and windows stayed put.

'The family kept going about their business and tried to ignore the cyclone. We didn't dare go outside, of course. Sometimes, objects flew past the windows or hit the walls with a thump. We always keep some stores of fish and provisions for times like this.

'When I got to the market this morning, its canvas roof was flapping in the wind, torn in places.'

Gideon was caught in the cyclone when he was in town. He told the class, 'The wind was very high and was blowing parts off buildings. I took shelter under the awning of a shop. The rain was pelting down and the water in the street was rising higher and higher. Soon people were wading up to their knees in water. Gradually, the water rose to our waists. Things were tripping people underfoot or were floating about, having come loose. We were lucky if we did not get hit by something flying through the air.

'I dashed to a house where the door was open. I found children and some old people standing in water. The children were standing on chairs. By luck, an empty boat drifted up to the house and got caught in the porch. I secured the boat and helped the family into it. Then I waited till more people came past who were able to guide the boat with me to a refuge on higher ground that was taking in stranded folk. After arriving at the community hall where people were sheltering, I crept around many sitting and lying on the floor, to see if I could be helpful. I squatted down to comfort those who were crying and had no companion.'

Noor said, 'My father was working in the hill country. You know he is an anthropologist. The wind and rain started up and he went to sit in his car. Soon, there was foliage, trees, coconuts falling down. Debris was flying about, like roofs, gates, and so on. It was dangerous. He decided he should try to drive home before it got worse. After he got a certain distance, he found the road was blocked by a mud slide. He knew there was a longer route and drove back to where it diverged. He managed to get home safely. Later, he heard that houses and a whole village had been buried by the mud slide. The community is trying to dig out the missing, possibly dead, people.'

The class members continued to tell their stories.

Sister Rosa said, 'Because of your tales of almost miraculous escapes from effects of the cyclone, listen while I tell you the miracle of the loaves and fishes. A multitude of people gathered to see Jesus when he was departing to go to a desert. He taught them many things, and it was late in the day and there was nothing to eat except five loaves of bread and two fishes. Jesus told the disciples to share the food among all the people, about five thousand of them, and they did. What are we to make of this story?'

Noor said, 'It's worthwhile to make even small offerings if you can, to those in need.'

Hannah said, 'We should share our food with the poor, and not waste it, as we often do.'

Sunny said, 'Yes, the solution to the problem of

hunger is to address it, whatever our resources.'

'Or any problem,' said Gideon.

Ayesha said, '"Where there's a will, there's a way." It's like my mother always says, "There's no such word as can't".'

'I'll add to that the thought of spiritual hunger and nourishment,' said Sister Rosa. 'You can share your faith, and pray, and accept God's assistance.' She always had the last word.

At the Friday meeting, Tomasin said, 'Jake and I went to a dance where people were drinking a lot of alcohol. I think it's a shame to get too drunk – it spoils the party for others. Why destroy your brain with alcohol. We should value our minds in order to enjoy life and do wonderful things in the world.'

Everyone agreed.

Noor said, 'We Muslims don't drink alcohol.'

Ayesha said, 'I never do, but not because I hold views about it. There's no alcohol at home. I don't go to parties and dances either.'

'Oh, Sunny and I do,' said Hannah, 'but we drink very little. Enough to fit in with the others. We see our parents drink too much and we don't like it.'

'Right on,' said Sunny, 'it's an embarrassment. I don't want to be like them.'

'Alcohol is a drug like any other drug,' said Jake, 'but people treat it as something different because of its long history of use in social settings. Did you know that King Henry the Eighth used to drink beer for breakfast. You had to drink alcohol instead of water in those days because water might make you sick.'

'Why didn't they boil it?' said Varsha.

'Because they didn't have the scientific knowledge. Science has changed the world.'

'And killed religion,' said Varsha.

'Well, obviously it hasn't,' said Jake, 'but it's rational to think it would. There are scientists who believe in God. They don't like to think of why that couldn't be.'

'Jake is giving the lectures this time, but I agree with him,' said Gideon. 'I drink in moderation like most adults do.'

The others agreed with this policy but weren't sure *most* adults did.

Gideon took Ayesha to a movie. She had never seen one. They sat at the back and held hands. Ayesha kept wondering who was playing the music or singing the songs. Why didn't it show them?

They went to see an exhibition of paintings of the Holy Madonna and Child. Ayesha liked especially the ones in which milk was squirting out of the mother's breasts.

'That happens in real life,' she said.

When they wandered together in the street, Ayesha loved to look in the windows of pet shops and toy shops. She had never had toys as a child. She picked up a knife or anything off the ground if she thought Ma could use it. Gideon bought her some scent, but she didn't like being given gifts. It made her feel she owed him something.

Gideon took Ayesha to a beach that was practically deserted during weekdays. He kissed her passionately and gradually drew off the clothes on her upper body. She did not push him away. He took off his shirt. She was resting back against a sandhill. He stroked her breasts with the tips of his fingers.

'They're soft like my mother's silk underwear,' he said. 'How beautiful you are.'

He put his cheek down and brushed it over her breast. She felt his eyelashes flicker on her skin, his lips.

'Your skin tastes salty like the sea.'

He raised his face and placed the palm of his hand over her nipple and moved it around.

'Your nipple has hardened and raised itself. The hollow of my palm is very sensitive, so it feels nice.'

Ayesha felt self-conscious and straightened up.

'Look, open your palm,' said Gideon. He stroked the centre.

'Ooh.'

He kissed her again and she felt his tongue between her lips. His hand pulled at her clothes.

'I don't want you to go farther down,' she said.

They chatted for a while or listened to the sea. He stroked the hair away from her face.

'You must have had a young love affair in Israel,' she said, 'because you knew about how a nipple would harden in the palm of your hand.'

'I did have a girlfriend, but it was a very innocent affair. We didn't go beyond what I did with you.'

'I don't feel very loved to think that. My body was

touched by deception at that moment. Now I'm conscious of the difference between my innocence and your experience.'

'Some women like men to have experience.'

'If they've had some experience themselves, I think.'

Does he still think of his old girlfriend, she wondered, perhaps longing to see her again, and planning to return to Israel. She became standoffish towards him.

The next time they had a date, Gideon took Ayesha on a trip to the hill country. They took a picnic lunch.

'I've heard of a river where there are rock pools you can swim in, and it's a nice place to have a picnic, cooler than down at the coast,' Gideon said.

It wasn't hard to find a spot by the river. Other people weren't there because it was a weekday. They saw a large rock pool surrounded by rocks. They sat on the rocks in the sun.

Gideon stripped down to his underpants. Ayesha did the same. They slipped into the water and swam around. Gideon was looking at her body. He came over to where she was and embraced her.

'Don't touch my breasts,' she said. It was enough that he looked at them.

They lay on the rocks after the swim, basking like lizards in the sun and drying out. Ayesha went to put on her clothes.

'Come and have our picnic,' she said.

They sat there quietly after eating, listening to the wind in the trees and noises of crickets and cicadas. They went for a walk through the trees. Gideon put his arms around Ayesha and kissed her. She enjoyed that.

Going to bed at home, she felt a warm glow in her heart. As she drifted towards sleep, *Princess Ayesha said: 'The sultan and I sailed back to his country. I would like to say I lived happily ever after, but my husband turned out to be a controlling type of person. Having made me a kind of prisoner to his wishes by marrying me, he continued to make me feel imprisoned in his castle, by not allowing me this or that freedom. He never abused me by physical violence, or shouted at me, or punished me, or used demeaning words, though. He truly loved me and gave me a place in his heart. I bore him a son and he was very happy. We lived a contented life. I sighed for loss of freedoms which were more imaginary than real, due to my chafing at his controlling manner.*

'He controlled my life so that no one in my family would know what had happened to me and would continue to reckon me dead. But by the time my son grew up, I think people knew whose grandson he was, and he became the leader of the Bajau people.'

'It was appropriate that he was,' said Ayesha, *'because, like the fisherman who rescued you, they had become sea-faring people!'*

CHAPTER 12

All the students had helped to arrange for the fete and fair at the showground. It was being held on the day of an annual Bajau celebration. Any person or group could come and give a talk about the work of their community or organisation. They could demonstrate their singing, dancing and cultural activities. They could bring their arts and crafts or anything to display and sell. There would be little stalls and amusements.

Ayesha got her friend Yasmin to go with her to the fete and fair, as their people were participating in it. Because of her other activities, Ayesha hadn't been seeing Yasmin as much as she once had.

'Our people are going to perform their ceremonies later under the giant fig tree,' said Ayesha.

They walked over to the tree in a corner of the showground to see what was there. Seated on the ground, some women were selling mats they wove; others were demonstrating mat-weaving. They had on sale jewellery made with pearls they had dived for. There were also wood carvings the men had done, and men carving them.

The Bajau horsemen, who lived on the land, had come dressed in their highly decorated costumes and tall hats they wore for special occasions. Their horses had decorated bridles and saddles too. They were giving pony rides to children.

Ayesha and Yasmin thought they would return later when the celebrations began. They found a hoopla. You had to throw a hoop onto a hook on a wall beside the prize you wanted to win. Ayesha hoped Yasmin would win something to take home. As it turned out, the hoop hooked itself beside the cap she'd aimed for, and she won a teddy.

'I'll give it to a young child I know,' she said. 'She's never had a toy.'

They ate a donut, then candy floss, and felt sick. They watched a monkey, dressed in clothes, perform tricks and ride a small bike.

'I feel sorry for the monkey,' said Ayesha.

Yasmin said, 'I think he enjoyed it.'

They went to a stall to have face-painting like the little kids, and also have stripes of rainbow colours sprayed on their hair.

'It makes us look gay,' said Yasmin.

'Do you know what that means?'

'Like happy.'

Ayesha explained what it was.

They caught sight of some baby farm animals and went over to the crowd of younger children who were reaching into the enclosures to pet them. It was a novelty for Ayesha and Yasmin, living on the ocean, to see baby animals; lambs, piglets, chicks and a calf. They were as thrilled as the children.

They were getting hungry and up ahead was a stall selling homemade cakes, jams and pickles. Some people were eating at tables. When they reached the stall, they saw Devonshire teas were being served.

'Scones, cream and jam,' read Ayesha. 'Let's have that for lunch.'

They were down to the last crumbs when Odin suddenly appeared.

'The Bajau will begin their ritual dancing and singing soon,' he said.

They walked with him back to the fig tree. Ayesha waved to Jake and Tomasin, who were holding hands. She said a friendly hello to Chris, who was on his own. She thought, Yasmin might like him. I'll take her to the drop-in centre sometime and introduce them.

Near the tree, the horsemen were now displaying different formations and movements with their horses. They carried spears. When the horses moved, the bells on their necks jingled loudly. Then the group went off to one side of the tree.

Ayesha, Yasmin and Odin sat on the grass with the large audience. The Bajau musicians came and sat at the base of the tree. They started to play their gongs, flutes, drums and a xylophone. The folk from the stilt houses entered from one side, singing and dancing as they circled the tree. They were dressed in their brightly coloured best clothes, with beads and embroidery, which they had sewn themselves. Many in the audience were watching them for the first time and were entranced.

It was a joyous celebration, with clapping and other movements of hands in time to the music. They were doing ritual trance dancing, in which they believed they were possessed by spirits of their ancestors. These benign spirits would leave their bodies when they stopped dancing.

After they finished, it was time for Ayesha's speech about the Jinn religion. Odin shushed the spectators and said Ayesha would give a short talk.

Ayesha stood up and said, 'I am a Bajau student of literacy at the convent. My family belong to a branch of Islam called Jinn. Jinn are spirits who rule the world. People's spirit controls their bodies. There are spirits of wind, storm, the sea, first rice harvest and so on. Jinn can take different forms. They have the same basic needs as humans. They can move fast and carry heavy objects but can't be seen. They can cause mental and physical harm to humans. They can cure mental illness. You can be possessed by a Jinn. People believed in these spirits before Christianity came.'

Tomasin, sitting with the audience on the grass, then stood up and said, 'I am partly American-Indian and my ancestors had religions that were like Jinn.'

Why isn't Gideon here? thought Ayesha. He was supposed to come.

Now Buddhist monks, with their bald heads and orange robes, shepherded by Hannah, walked in a line to sit under the fig tree. They had musical instruments with them. While the audience quietened down, they began a hum of 'om' for meditation, which the audience copied. They stopped and waited for silence. Taking up their cymbals, clapping sticks, drums and trumpets, they played on the instruments and chanted from religious texts, which was their kind of praying. After some time, the performance reached its end.

Hannah stood up and said, 'The monks will be serving everyone with a free lunch after my talk. I am a Buddhist. We are followers of a real man who lived a long time ago; Buddha. He travelled around as a young man, sitting under trees and meditating on his experience of life. As a result of this, he found enlightenment, which is a balance of wisdom and compassion, law and love. He believed in the Good (the *Buddha*) which is in all people, who must find it in themselves. He pursued a middle way of life, neither one of luxury nor of poverty. The middle way is the cure to suffering, by eliminating selfish desire. It is a way of intuition, which rejects discrimination. It leads to new birth, tolerance and serenity. People concentrate on living in the present moment. They practise non-attachment, which releases them from desire and gives them a heightened perspective on life. You know Buddhists believe in reincarnation. I would like to come back as a male, in my next life. People are sometimes Buddhist as well as belonging to another religion because there is no important conflict of belief. Some people in this country were Buddhists before Christianity came.'

'Do you have any questions?'

Yasmin whispered to Ayesha, 'Why are their robes orange?'

'I don't know.' She grabbed Yasmin's hand, put it up and nudged her. 'Go on, ask.'

'Why are their robes orange?' Yasmin said loudly to Hannah.

'It was the only dye available at the time they started up,' said Hannah. 'You probably thought there was a religious reason.'

Yasmin nodded. The monks had meanwhile carried in the pots of food they had cooked for the multitude. Sunny told everyone to stay sitting on the ground and the monks would go around with servings of their delicious rice and vegetable stew, with fish they had bought from the Bajau. Much to their surprise, the lunch came on a banana leaf as a plate. They had to eat with their hands.

Ayesha left Yasmin with the other Bajau and went to a meeting of the 'People Against Dynamite Fishing'. On the way, she saw Jihad, but he had grown a beard so she wasn't sure. He was with another man who also had a beard. She pretended she hadn't seen them.

At the dynamite fishing meet, there was quite a roll up. She sat on a chair at the back. The proceedings were about to begin, and there was a hush.

'Welcome,' said a woman who appeared to be the main speaker. 'We are here today to consider the damage to our oceans and fish stocks from dynamite fishing. Dynamite fishing is usually carried out by poorer people who can't afford the equipment used for commercial fishing. But this kind of fishing is killing fish that are not even eaten because most sink to the ocean floor after the explosion. Only some fish float to the surface after the blast, where they are easy to pick up. Dynamite fishing is steadily reducing the number of fish in the ocean. So all fishermen are finding they have fewer and fewer fish to sell. This reduction will be felt mostly by poor people. Of course, dynamite fishing is banned by law, but it is not being strictly enforced. We must lobby the government more about this matter.'

'Isn't dynamite fishing also killing turtles and destroying fish eggs, and the plankton that fish eat?' said a man.

'Yes, killing off the coral reefs they live in,' said the speaker. 'It is damaging whales and dolphins too.'

'What about the effects of climate change?' said a woman. 'Isn't that reducing the numbers of fish?'

'Yes, and of their food sources also. So there is a double whammy, of dynamite fishing and climate change.'

Ayesha said, 'All life in the sea is a gift of God and should be treasured.'

The audience applauded.

Someone said, 'Aren't you a Bajau girl? They are the worst offenders.'

'I am Bajau. But my family don't do dynamite fishing. Our people need to know more about it so they can consider not doing it. But I believe it's the only way some can make a decent living.'

'And get killed or injured through homemade bombs exploding?' said a woman.

'Look, you can't blame me for everything the Bajau do, as if I were responsible for it. I don't blame you personally for murderers, thieves and other criminals in your society, do I?

'Stop picking on me because I am Bajau. I'm sick of the constant and unfair verbal attacks I've had as I go about my life. I would try to stop dynamite fishing if I could.'

Ayesha got up and walked away. She thought someone might shout something rude at her as she left, but there was deadly silence.

There was another meeting she wanted to attend. There, a speaker took the stand for a speech on drugs.

'I am talking about the use of illicit drugs, not medicines that make you well. I want to prevent the use of these drugs. The government is trying to stop drug trafficking. Don't take these drugs. They will destroy your life, affecting your physical and mental health, your job, your family, your future. You can get hooked, enslaved, by a drug. To pay for it, you may commit crimes – theft, prostitution, murder. The streets become unsafe. You can get free help to give up drugs. Ask at the drop-in centre, or hospital, or ask a doctor.'

Ayesha thought, I remember a man selling drugs in the yard at the back of the drop-in centre. She went to find Yasmin again, as they were going to finish their day at the fair watching a display of Olympic wrestling. I didn't see Gideon. Why didn't he come?

CHAPTER 13

Ayesha walked to Gideon's place, and his mother opened the door.

'Is Gideon at home?' said Ayesha.

'Yes. Come in.' His mother called him and showed Ayesha into the lounge room. When Gideon came, she left them to it.

Ayesha said, 'Why didn't you come to the fair, if you don't mind my asking?'

'I had something to tell you which I didn't want to say there. My old girlfriend in Israel wrote to me, and we've been writing to each other since.'

'So you feel you're having a relationship with her again.'

'Yes. For the time being.'

'Well, thanks for telling me now.'

Ayesha had often seen rubbish along the sea shore, going back and forth in the canoe. She got the other students to go with her to the jetty and see for themselves. They were shocked by it.

'This plastic is being ingested by fish and birds and killing them,' said Noora.

'None of this rubbish is from our group,' said Ayesha. 'We don't eat food from tins or glass or plastic containers.'

They organized a day to meet there and try to collect as much rubbish as possible. Most of it was plastic.

Everyone walked there with a large garbage bin to put the rubbish in, and they started work. Further along the shore, they were confronted by a crocodile with wide-open mouth!

They shouted and threw stones at it, and it went away into the water with a swish of its tail.

'We're lucky to have seen one,' said Ayesha. 'They are rarely seen here.'

It was an overwhelming job. They agreed to return regularly to pick up trash on different parts of the shore, and to bring more people with them. Then, when the bins were full, everyone went home.

Ayesha sometimes saw people scrounging for food in garbage bins in the street as she walked her usual routes between the jetty, the market, the convent and the drop-in centre. These hungry people were able to find food to eat immediately, like takeaways that had become throwaways. It was unhygienic and might make them sick. But it gave Ayesha the idea that perhaps more waste was occurring in businesses and factories.

She found out where a big garbage dump was and went there. What a sight it was, with mobs of people, including children, stumbling, crawling and poking their way through the rubbish, in competition with a host of birds, to find treasures to keep or sell. Clearly, they found food to eat all day in doing so.

'Do you come here often?' Ayesha enquired of a woman.

'Yes. This is my family business. I and my children live over there.' She pointed to a tarpaulin draped over some boxes. 'We mainly find things at night so that we can sell them during the day. We sell to people like you on the spot.'

'I don't have any money,' said Ayesha.

As she wandered about the edges of the dump, she wondered if this was the best way to distribute waste. It wouldn't be, because young mothers or sick, injured or elderly people would be unable to come and scrounge. It was an unhealthy place anyway. I'll need to go to cafes, factories and other places to find out how much waste they have and what they are doing with it, she thought.

Ayesha arranged to go to a hotel with Jake to see how they managed to reduce waste. They felt someone on the hotel staff might have more time to answer their questions than the staff in a busy restaurant.

'They would both have the same procedures,' said Jake.

They asked the receptionist if they could see the manager. 'What for?' she said.

'We want to find out how you deal with food waste for our project,' said Ayesha. 'We're students from the convent.'

'Okay, he would have time for that. I'll take down your names.' She wrote them, and then called the manager on the internal phone.

'Aah, he'll see you in about half an hour. Sit over there on the comfortable chairs.'

It was a longer wait than they expected. At last the

manager came to listen to their questions. He sat down.

'Do you have a program for keeping waste in your business at the lowest level you can?' said Ayesha.

'Yes, we do. First, we conduct a food waste audit. This keeps track of what's being wasted, why it's thrown out and how much. I'll give you all this on a sheet of info we have. We try to avoid wasting any ingredients before they're prepared, so we record how long food is being stored, and make sure there is no over-ordering. We have a plan for how to use leftovers the next day by altering the menu.'

He paused. Ayesha stared at him. A flicker of recognition crossed his face. She suddenly remembered that this man had said something nasty to her once at the market. I can't let that pass, she thought.

'Didn't you revile me once at the market?' I'm taking courage by being with Jake. 'Say nasty things?'

'No, I did not.' He looks guilty, she thought.

He continued, 'Getting back to my account, we also try to gauge what size portions of food our customers like, while we're also investigating the popularity of different dishes. We make our kitchen team aware of waste and get them to think how things are done in the kitchen. We also compost scraps by sending them to another place.'

'Do you ever donate them to a charity?' said Ayesha. 'Jesus said, "Gather up the leftover fragments of food that nothing may be lost".'

'I take your point. We would consider it. Actually, we're wasting very little as it is.'

'Our project requires action on our behalf,' said Jake.

'We were thinking how we could deliver waste food to poor people. But we don't usually have vehicles to transport it.'

'I commend you for your intentions,' said the manager.

'Maybe you should think of doing it,' said Ayesha. 'You could contact charitable organizations and find out how much they are already doing in this field.'

'If they could send a representative to talk to us about a plan of distributing our food waste, we would certainly listen to it, and go from there.'

'It would be a good idea,' said Jake, 'for us to get charities to do this with hotels and restaurants, and we could coordinate it.'

'That wouldn't be easy for students to do,' said the manager. 'It'd be better if they came direct to us.'

'Yes, I see,' said Ayesha. 'But thank you for helping us work all this out. We'll talk with people in the charities.'

'What about non-food waste?' cut in Jake hastily, before the manager ended the interview.

'You mean plastic and paper? We've cut down or banned our use of them. We use china cups and no straws or sachets of tea, coffee, sugar and powdered milk. We give water to our guests in glass jugs, and we use cotton laundry bags. The chefs have to avoid paper or plastic packaging.'

'Thank you,' said Jake. 'We have to write a report and will send you a copy.'

'We'll interview more people like you,' said Ayesha.

Jake wrote down some notes quickly about non-food

waste as they were leaving.

Ayesha said, 'He did revile me and he lied by denying it, like Judas. So nothing he said can be trusted as true. He knows all the stuff to say about waste, but is he doing it? He should have admitted his wrongdoing to me and said sorry.'

'Aren't you asking too much? He's saving face,' said Jake. 'Why do you go on and on about being reviled?'

'You just don't understand it, do you, from your position of privilege. For years and years, I just felt it and said nothing. Now I've made a bold change of direction.

'What about your addiction to alcohol when you were a child? Surely it caused you harm and had repercussions in your life.'

'Yes. I've faced up to them since.'

'Well, you should have some empathy for me.'

Ayesha did not expect to hear from her again soon, but the princess came back and said: 'We had a good life, but my husband took to keeping concubines, which means he had sex with other women. He gave them apartments to live in, fine clothes and food delicacies as a kind of payment.'

'I wouldn't like that,' said Ayesha.

'It was the custom in this country, for rich men. I tolerated it as I was happy living my own life. I enjoyed bringing up my son and teaching him all the things he should know about the world. I told him he should not take for granted the good fortune he had in his life. I revived my interests in art and music and shared them with my son. We enjoyed having pets, and horses to ride. I also did work

for poor people and set him an example of charitable activities. My son learned to be like me and not a controlling person like his father.'

'But you did not have a good enough life,' said Ayesha.

'Who are you to say that? Perfection is only in God, and as an idea in the human mind. It drives every animal as it listens to its stomach. But it cannot be reached in this life.'

One evening, when Ayesha was walking to the jetty, she saw in front of her two men making some sort of exchange. In the late afternoon light, with the sun shining in her eyes, she couldn't see what it was. The dark beards suggested they were jihadists. Suddenly, police appeared.

'Pull the girl out of the way,' said one of them.

Ayesha shrugged off the policeman's hands and walked on quickly but looked back to see what was happening. The police grabbed the two men, and they had a scuffle. One man fell to the ground and the other started running. One of the police drew his gun and shot the running man. Then he turned his gun towards the man on the ground and shot him too.

Omar suddenly appeared as if from nowhere, and said, 'Don't be afraid. These men were wanted for crimes. Of course, the police shouldn't shoot them, they are corrupt. The men should be brought before the law.' He escorted her to her canoe.

She said, 'I was all right.'

Omar said, 'I want to become an imam, like a priest.

I will have to look after people and protect them from harm if I can.'

Ayesha gradually found out more terrible things the jihadists did. She tried to persuade Jihad not to follow them.

CHAPTER 14

One morning, when Ayesha was paddling to the shore, she looked up at the sky and saw that the clouds appeared exactly like the sea, the average sort of peaks and troughs. Then she looked towards the horizon, but it was so blurry that the sky and sea seemed to be one, in a palette of grey. It was like she was in an air bubble with sea all around it. Reaching the jetty, she was glad to step out into her normal world.

She was working on more reports about waste. She found Varsha and asked if she'd like to go with her to see what food was wasted by supermarkets and grocery shops.

Varsha said, 'Yes *please*. I thought I'd learn better English and meet people in the class, but I didn't expect to be able to participate in research.'

When Ayesha and Varsha walked into a supermarket, they asked for the manager. After a while, a man turned up who said he was in charge of ordering. 'The manager is not onsite.'

Ayesha said, 'We're students doing a project on waste. We want to know what you waste.'

'We're trying to do something about waste. It's common in supermarkets to throw away fruit and veg that's not a standard size or shape. For instance, a banana that is too curved or a potato that's an odd shape, harder to peel. Actually, farmers are now trying to grow straight bananas. Customers don't like fruit or veg that is too small or too large.'

'I always look for fruit that is small,' said Ayesha.

'But you are not typical. Or they don't like fruit that is bruised. But bruising doesn't matter, the fruit will taste as good. Also, too much plastic is used in shops. Things are being wrapped more than in the past and come into shops already in plastic wrapping.'

'Should you be doing more?' said Varsha.

'Yes, definitely. We are overstocking food and have misleading sell-by dates. We should sell the rejected food, or use it in making prepared meals, or donate it to charities, or compost it. You should ask farmers also about how they deal with unwanted food.'

'Oh, we hadn't thought of that!' said Ayesha. 'We're going to ask some householders about their food wastage too.'

Other students decided to find out what food people wasted at home, so they asked their parents about it or observed it themselves. Generally, their parents were aware of the problem and tried not to waste food. They ate up leftovers and did not allow food to sit around going bad.

'If you went to other's houses, you might see a lot of waste,' said the twin's mother. 'Researchers are doing studies of it.'

Ayesha was now aware of waste of food by the very farmers who grew it. She enlisted the help of Gideon again to take her in his family's car to pay a visit to the farmer they had met earlier on his farm. He seemed keen to go with her and was affectionate. Something's changed again, she thought.

Arriving at the gate, they saw the farmer still had a sign up for tomatoes for sale, and drove in.

'Do you remember us?' Ayesha said, as the farmer came into sight.

'I think I do. Weren't you the students who asked me whether I treasured my God-given farm?'

'Yes,' said Ayesha and Gideon both together, laughing. 'We've come to buy more tomatoes and to ask more questions.'

'Well, here's a basket to pick the tomatoes first.'

When they had picked a good pile of them, they returned to pay the farmer, who was cleaning his tractor in the shed.

'Now, what do you wish to ask me?'

'It's about wasting food,' said Ayesha. 'We've been going around supermarkets and restaurants asking about waste for a project we're doing at the convent. Do you waste any of what you produce on the farm?'

'I sometimes throw stuff away or feed it to the stock.'

'What are you throwing out?'

'Fruit that has gone bad or is bruised. Sometimes, it is a strange size or shape that I know the supermarkets don't like, but we eat those ones.'

'How do you feel about discarding it?'

'Well, mostly it's warranted. It's okay if the animals eat it, and actually I'm throwing it in the compost heap. So really I don't feel it's being wasted.'

'I think you're right.'

On the way home, Gideon told Ayesha that his old girlfriend he'd been writing to in Israel had suddenly stopped writing.

He said, 'Can I see you again?'

'Yes.' They went to have coffee.

Ayesha said, 'I was brought up to think of being married when I grew up. Nothing about having relationships with a boy in my teenage years, or before marriage.'

'Most Israeli girls would think like that too. Their parents rub it into them. But boys still try to be their boyfriends.'

'So now you are lacking a girlfriend?'

'I'll say.'

'Do you think that's just about sex?'

'No. But the prospect of sex with that girl is always on one's mind.'

This made Ayesha blush.

It was Friday, and time for the weekly meeting of the students at the convent. It was often Hannah who led discussions.

She said, 'It was an eye-opener for me to observe how much food was wasted in our house. Sunny and I were the worst. I'm more aware now of poor people in the world who don't have enough food. I should be thinking what to do about it.'

'I've offered to keep an eye on everything in the fridge and seeing that it's eaten up,' said Noor.

'On another subject at home,' said Varsha, 'I've

offered to keep my room tidier – I tend to be messy and leave clothes lying around. I'm also going to do more chores now Mum has a part-time job. I'm trying to get my little bro to help, but he doesn't accept my authority.'

Tomasin said, 'At home, I tend to shut myself in my room and feel lonely. I'm shutting out my mother, who hurts my feelings. Dad works long hours sometimes and I think Mum misses his company. I do volunteer to cook dinner twice a week and Mum has to keep out of the kitchen.'

'I feel lonely at times because of being an only child whose parents have high expectations of,' said Gideon, 'waiting to be a grown-up. As for cooking, I plead guilty. My mother won't let me do it – it's *her* job. She's old-fashioned.'

'I can empathize with waiting to grow up,' said Sunny. 'I'm tired of waiting – it seems so long. I cook if I feel like it.'

Ayesha said, 'We don't ever waste food. I have few belongings to leave in a mess. I'm ashamed to admit Mum does nearly all the housework. It's her recognized responsibility.

'I was watching videos on the computer and felt embarrassed about things I saw and heard – not used to them in my life. So I stopped watching them.'

'Nothing wrong with that!' said Jake. 'It's good we listen to one another's problems.'

One day, Ayesha took a break out the back of the drop-in centre where people went to smoke a cigarette.

A man came up to her and said, 'Take a puff on my cigarette and see if you like it.'

'I don't smoke.'

'But this is a completely different type of cigarette. Take a puff and see.'

She took a puff and coughed. She wasn't used to it. Then a very nice feeling washed over her. 'I see what you mean.'

She stood around, watching the man smoke. He gave her another puff.

'If you would like to buy these, they are more expensive than ordinary cigarettes. You only buy one at a time, but their effects last a lot longer.'

'I don't have spare money for cigarettes. How much are they?'

The man told her a price. He asked if she had that amount on her. Ayesha realized she was holding more than that sum from selling the fish at the market, but she had to buy fruit, vegetables and provisions with it later in the afternoon.

'I'll think about it and tell you later.'

The man shrugged and walked away.

When Ayesha was confronted by the man again another day, he said, 'I've brought pills this time, which work the same way as my special cigarettes. You won't have to smoke it, just swallow it.'

'Oh, I could take that without my friends knowing I've done something unusual for me.'

I'll buy one to see what's it's like, she thought. I could buy cheaper, smaller, and less fruit and veg. I'll tell Ma the price has gone up. She bought a pill to experiment with on a rainy day.

In the morning, Ayesha was woken up by a blast that rocked the house. It sounded like a terrific explosion of dynamite nearby. They all rushed outside to see boats racing away from the site.

'Some dynamite has been deliberately set off near to our house,' said Dad.

Soon after, they saw dead fish rising to the surface of the water. Of course, Dad went out in the boat to collect them.

'That was meant to give us a fright,' said Dad, 'but they have targeted the wrong people.'

'I've had threats perpetually from an anti-dynamite fishing group,' said Ayesha, 'but I didn't say anything as I didn't want to worry you. They know me by sight around town and have tracked me down to where I live. I was noticeable especially at the fete when I spoke about the matter.'

Gran was crying so they had to comfort her.

Ayesha was resting on the veranda when a huge pelican alighted on the railings. It flapped its wings and clapped its bill, emitting a rattling noise in the skin pouch below its throat that was vibrating. Ayesha kept quiet and still so as not to frighten it off. But it suddenly dived into the water.

It's catching the dead fish that were bombed and are rising to the surface, thought Ayesha. The pelican returned to the railing. Holding its open bill up, it made swallowing motions and a fish disappeared down its throat. Then it spread its wings and flew away.

A shot rang out. Why is someone shooting pelicans? she thought.

CHAPTER 15

Ayesha had lunch with Chris at the drop-in centre. She hadn't seen him lately.

She said, 'Would you like to go with me to see what food is wasted in a hospital?'

He said, 'Yes. Actually, I've been there recently to have a check-up for my cancer – it hasn't returned.'

'Oh. I'm so glad.'

When they entered the foyer of the hospital, they managed to pin down a staffer to explain the object of their mission.

She said, 'Hi there, Chris, I remember you. We're now practising something that's been researched elsewhere. We only serve patients food on demand and in this manner, we save thirty per cent of the food that would have been wasted. We're very glad of this as we're not a rich country.'

'I've heard hospitals sometimes use washable gowns and sometimes disposable ones,' said Ayesha. 'Which is cheapest?'

'In the long run, the washable ones are, so we stick with them.'

'Do you counsel patients who might be distressed by the situation they're in?' said Chris.

'We certainly do. By the way, congrats on the

research you're both doing. It's called "action research" because it can lead to change being made.'

Heading home afterwards, Ayesha said, 'Did you have counselling when you were there?'

'Yes, I never told you. They care about the mental health of patients.'

Chris had accompanied her to the jetty. They said goodnight and he turned for home.

The next time Ayesha met Chris at the drop-in centre, they talked about their lives.

Chris said, 'I was born and grew up on a farm. Many people live in rural areas. I went to the regional school which doesn't go to the end of secondary school. I was lucky because farming folk are usually quite poor. They can't pay for their children's transport, uniforms and school expenses, though schools are free. So, many children don't go to school but work on the farm to help their family. Later, they become dropouts, selling things on the street like cigarettes, candy, garlands and foodstuffs. Some become beggars.'

'So I'm not alone in lacking secondary school then,' said Ayesha.

'No, and I would like to complete secondary school and do the exams. It would make me better at running a business.'

He said he had seen Ayesha talking to the drug dealer at the back of the drop-in centre. He already knew what was going on there. He said, 'Ayesha, don't take any drug you may have bought from the dealer. It will harm you and affect your life. You would be spending your food money on it.'

'Do you know what suffering I have had in my short life?'

'I know from having had cancer. I'm still recovering, and it might come back. It's because of suffering that I have sympathy for you. It would tear my heart to see you taking this drug.'

'Why should you care about it?'

'I just do. Because I like you.'

At the Friday meeting, Hannah, the self-appointed chairperson, said, 'I notice Jake and Tomasin act a bit lovey-dovey these days.'

'What, us?' the two culprits said, eyebrows raised.

'Gideon and I have been seeing each other,' said Ayesha.

'I wasn't going to say anything,' said Gideon.

Noor said she had her eye on a certain person who was her friend. 'What about you, Hannah?'

'I have the same,' said Hannah coyly.

'Not I,' said Sunny.

Varsha said, 'I would like to have a boyfriend.'

'I'll find you someone,' said Hannah.

'No, it would have to happen naturally. Otherwise, it would be like something arranged. I don't mind a blind date.'

'All right,' said Hannah. 'I'll try to find two men, so they won't feel too put upon, and we'll all go out on a double date.'

'Yes, that would be nice,' said Varsha.

Ayesha was always wanting to have more discussions with Ma and spend time with her.

She said to her one day, 'I wish I knew more about the Bajau people who became farmers and horsemen.'

Ma said, 'I've often wondered about them and was pleased to see the horsemen at the fete.'

'I think I know a way we could go and meet them. My friend Noor said once her father might take us to visit some of them.'

When she next had the opportunity, Ayesha went to Noor's place and asked her about it.

Noor said, 'Oh yes, I remember. Dad knows some Bajau farmers who live on farms in the hill country where he studies the tribes. I'll ask him if he has time now to take us there.'

Later, at the market, Noor turned up and said, 'Dad knows a farmer we can meet and talk with and has arranged to take us all to visit him. We can all fit in the car. Can you come to our house on Saturday after the market?'

'Yes, and it will suit Ma and Dad too.'

Ayesha walked with her mum and dad to Noor's on Saturday. Smoke had blanketed the town. She pointed out to her parents that it was from the annual burning off of pine forests in the hills, which farmers did for land clearing. There were more fires around too because of climate change.

Ayesha introduced her parents. Ma and Dad were to sit in the back with Noor.

'Won't you be too squashed?' Ayesha said to Noor.

'No, and we want you to sit in the front to see the view and talk with Dad,' said Noor.

Noor's dad drove them up the winding mountain roads in the ever smokier conditions.

'It's not dangerous as I know these roads well and the fires are not out of control,' he said, slowing the car. 'Look, a wild deer! They are endangered.'

'Do you know children in town say that hamburgers are made out of endangered animals,' said Ayesha.

'That's nonsense.'

They came to a humble-looking farmhouse near to the road and went up the drive. The farmer left his work to welcome them. They could sit and talk at the outside table.

'It's good of you to talk with us,' said Noor's dad. 'This is my daughter Noor and her friend Ayesha and her family.'

Ayesha's ma and dad shook hands with the man and said they were Bajau people who lived on the coast.

Ayesha said, 'My father is a fisherman and we live in a stilt house. I didn't know about our people who branched into farming. I'm making studies of our people for a project. I'm very interested in them.'

'What would you like to know?'

'Did you come from a fishing family?'

'Yes. When I was a child. My father decided to make a break to farming because he had a friend who had done it and could show him the ropes.'

'How did he cope with the new way of living?'

'With difficulty and hard work. The Bajau farmers

have the poorest land as they are late comers. They were able to purchase at low prices remnants of pine forest that were not part of a reserve. They've had to chop down and burn the forest – as you can see by the smoke at present.'

'Do other farmers treat you as equals?'

'More or less. Behind our backs, they blame us for things, like fires getting away onto others' land. In reality, these accidental fires can be caused by any farmer. We hear about their complaints because their children pass them on at school to our children.'

'I am reviled unjustly by people in town who recognize me as Bajau, and I'm blamed for things my family don't do, like dynamite fishing.'

'Of course we don't do that,' said Dad, looking horrified.

'We get some discrimination against us here,' said the farmer. 'They look down on us because we are new to farming and have the poorest land.'

'Do you have any horse-riding Bajau here?' said Ma.

'No. They have farms on flat land suitable for horses, as horses go lame on steep blocks like ours.'

They chatted on and found out that the farmer's children were allowed to go to school because they had birth certificates and lived on the land. Besides, the small community needed them at school so that they could keep up the numbers; otherwise, they risked the government closing the school if enrolments got too low.

Noor's dad took everyone to have lunch at a café he knew in the hills, and Ayesha rated it the best lunch she'd ever had; it was homemade with local recipes and produce.

Her mum and dad said how much they valued the trip and learning about the Bajau farmer doing so well in life. It was a real treat for them to drive up into the hill country. They hardly ever did things together.

When they came home, Ayesha told Ma and Dad about how Princess Ayesha of long ago said the tribe had once lived on the land, but they went to live at sea after a calamity. The princess was lost on the way to meeting her future husband, and the king was angry because his people failed to find her. Later, some of them returned to the land.

'How do you know all this?' asked Ma.

'I must have read it in the convent library.'

One evening after dark, Ayesha and Gideon were making love on the back seat of his family car in a park. Ayesha had taken the pill she'd bought at the drop-in centre, but she didn't tell Gideon about it. She felt light-headed and ecstatic. A bright light suddenly shone on them. They sat up hastily, Gideon pulling up his trousers and Ayesha pulling down her skirt to hide the fact that she had no underpants on.

'Police!' a man called. He came over and tapped on the window next to Gideon, who opened the door of the car and said, 'We're all right.'

'The girl too?'

'I'm okay,' said Ayesha.

'Don't you two do anything rash,' said the policeman, and left straight away.

Ayesha and Gideon lost their taste for lovemaking because of the intervention of the police and went home.

Ayesha realized that by taking the drug, she had been careless about what she was doing with Gideon. She might have got pregnant if they'd gone on.

Gideon had asked her to use a contraceptive, but she said she wasn't ready for it. She felt that using contraceptives seemed like a loss of her innocence. She didn't want to be knowing about such things, intending to make love. She wanted it to happen spontaneously.

'About what we were doing in the car the other evening,' said Ayesha. 'I don't want to have sex before I'm married. I could have become pregnant before the police arrived. The police saved me. I don't want to get pregnant, and I don't want to take contraceptives, and your parents don't want you to marry me.'

'I don't have to do what my parents say, but I'm too young to get married. I will be going to university, perhaps in another country.'

'So let's just be friends.'

'It looks like that's the only option. Look, Ayesha, I really fell in love with you whole-heartedly, and couldn't imagine ever being without you. Maybe that's what first love is like. It was as if we were married on the spot and couldn't be parted.'

'Yes, I felt it too. It was sudden and over-whelming. I kept holding onto you as if it was forever. When our lips met to kiss, they stayed like that. Time stood still.'

'I don't think we are a good love match though. We're both too dominating.'

CHAPTER 16

Ayesha saw again at the back of the drop-in centre, the man who sold her a pill. She felt herself being drawn to him although she had a feeling of foreboding. She knew she shouldn't buy it and take it, at the cost of her family's diet. She was deceiving them and it was wrong and she felt guilty. But the man attracted her attention and she walked up to him. He immediately took out a pill.

'I have a pill here for you.'

'I might try one again, though I shouldn't. Just one.' She bought it.

Soon after taking the pill, Ayesha had a feeling of lightness as if she were floating or hardly touching the ground and was about to fly away like a bird. I am light-headed, she thought.

She was in a plane with her hero Leonardo da Vinci, who had invented a flying machine. He had invented the parachute, a tank, a robot, a calculator, the odometer to measure distance and had made drawings of human anatomy and babies in the womb.

'The sun does not move,' he said.

Ayesha was looking down at the world and telling him about all the things that had changed since his time. She felt his wonder and awe magnified a thousand times.

She went tripping down the street to a park and swung

on the swings like a younger child. She climbed a tree and sat in the branches like a bird. The tree was shaking itself as though it had a head of hair it was drying.

I am happy and carefree, she thought, light-hearted. This is my feeling of lightness.

She forgot about going to her class. She had no wish to be with other people. She wanted to play. She was on a magic carpet riding high over the world. The carpet held and cuddled her like she was a baby. She chuckled and screamed with delight.

Later, she talked to Hannah about her lightness because Hannah noticed a difference in her. Ayesha didn't mention taking a drug. She said she was becoming more herself and it was just the bumps of growing up, even if she had to start back in childhood. She hadn't been through adolescent rebellion and had had to be more grown up than was suitable for her age, taking responsibility for adults in her family. She had had a heavy cross to bear because she was Bajau. Now she was recognizing it.

Hannah said perhaps Ayesha's lightness was like that in a book she'd read about the unbearable lightness of being. The unbearable part was having to think about the past and the future and being responsible. Ayesha said she'd never read the book, but her lightness was not unbearable, far from it, and not about being responsible.

I don't know what she's talking about, thought Ayesha, but I don't mind. These students are always talking about things I don't understand.

'Do you mean lightness as opposed to heavy… or dark?' said Hannah.

'Both.'

'Well, I can understand you in a different way. It is like the Buddhist way of living in the present. There is no past or future but only this moment in which you are experiencing everything just as it is. Doing this, you develop a heightened awareness of life.'

The third time Ayesha took a pill, she went to the park again. As she walked around, she felt she was walking on water because the ground was moving up and down like a swell. This was the same as the land-sickness the Bajau sometimes talked about. When they stepped out of their boats which were moving up and down, they felt the land was doing it too. You could feel giddy from it. She lay down on the ground and felt the swell under her, but it wouldn't make her sick this way.

I'm not feeling the heavy weight of my life now. I didn't realize what it would be like. I don't have to go on grieving about Dido. I didn't know that. I am not my brother's keeper.

But she was walking along the edge of an abyss. If she put one foot wrong, she would fall into the everlasting darkness. Sometimes, she did not inhabit herself, but was looking down at herself from the outside.

She was swallowed by a huge fish. She saw herself go down its gullet and through the stomach, then its bowel, winding this way and that with lots of little fish, where she fought demons. At last, she was expelled from its body and she swam home.

She went home with the provisions quite late. As she drew nearer to the house, she perceived a light moving across the water. Close to the landing, she saw a human form illuminated in the bright spot. It was Christ walking on the water! He could really do that. *He plants his footsteps in the sea and rides upon the storm.*

She stood up in the canoe and held out her arms and the lighted figure enveloped her. Sleepiness overwhelmed her. I must get into the house, she thought.

In the morning, Ma came into her room.

'You didn't eat the food I left out for you. All the provisions were still in the boat.'

Ayesha sat up.

'Look, you're sopping wet,' said Ma.

'I must have fallen in the water.' She thought, I must have tried walking on the water.

'You lay all night in your wet clothes. You were so tired!'

'A spirit boat took me away. I escaped and luckily I didn't drown.'

It wasn't difficult to carry out her usual duties of selling the fish and buying the provisions because they were a well-learnt routine. She told Ma she would clean the windows, which Ma didn't do very often, and she went on doing it, cleaning the same windows again and again, till Ma said to stop. A fly on the window told her, 'People think we are dirty, but we are clean, always washing ourselves.'

When she was coming off the effects of the drug for the day, she felt bad about squashing little insects that had no ability to save themselves against a great giant. Maybe they were humans who had been reincarnated. Seagulls kept tapping on the windows and annoying her.

She sometimes returned to her class. She sat there quietly and didn't speak. She left quickly afterwards. One day, she saw a huge black spider crawl over Sister Rosa. She giggled. Her classmates gave her dirty looks.

Sister Rosa said, 'Don't come to class in an inebriated state.'

Ayesha saw Sister Rosa rising up from the dead. Jesus said to her, in her head, 'Let the dead bury their dead'.

Ayesha was surprised at the market one day, sitting on a hessian bag with her fish spread out before her, when Noor turned up and said she'd come to see if she was all right.

'You haven't been to the classes for a while, and Hannah told me she saw you and you were different in some way and looked gaunt and unkempt. How are you?'

'I've been tired and not eating much. My skin doesn't feel good and I'm always scratching it. A nerve in my eye keeps twitching. I believe Jinn are inside me, causing illness. But I'm okay, just not up to doing classes. I spend my time at the drop-in centre.'

'You are shivering, and it's warm.' Noor spread out her hands in a what-can-I-do expression and went off.

Ayesha was sitting in the street, leaning against a building. She had taken a pill. A policeman came by and said, 'You are a drug addict, aren't you. Get up and go before I arrest you.'

When she got home, Mum said, 'Grump died when you were in town today.'

'Oh, Grump. Grump. Oh.'

'He was very old. He passed away peacefully in his sleep. Gran sometimes thinks he is still with us. She goes into her room, and comes out and says, "I can't find Grump". I have to remind her of his death reassuringly. She says "Oh yes" but a bit later, I hear her talking to him. No harm is done by it. She will get used to it.'

Ayesha saw blood on Grump's blanket where he died. Mum said, 'The blood will gradually wash out.'

When the drug was wearing off each time, Ayesha felt guilt about Grump's death. I killed him. I bought cheaper fruit and veg, and less of them. She was haunted by his death. She knew that in Jinn belief, the soul of the dead sometimes returned to the world. She became frightened of Hell and the ancestral voices, and of being grabbed from behind.

She had thought of something new about Dido. He might have caught his foot in the rocks and been unable to free it. It would be like Dido, with his clumsiness and hyperactivity. Dad wouldn't have noticed it soon enough. Dido had been stuck there, unable to get help from his family. His body had never floated up to the surface. She felt she was to blame. She cried.

She was getting tired of the after effects of the drug. On the street, cars were monsters, roaring, and coming to eat her. If she took more pills she would be all right, but she could only afford one a day. If that.

She decided she would have to give up the drug, so she asked someone at the drop-in centre about somewhere to go for help. They referred her to a special drug therapy clinic. The people there would see her even if she was

Bajau and wouldn't judge her or report her to the authorities.

When Ayesha went for therapy, she was first seen on her own by a therapist who said her name was Zoe. Zoe said she was right to come.

Ayesha said, 'Even a Bajau person who has no rights.'

'Yes, even more so. Always ask for me by name – and any time in the future.'

'I'm trying to recover from being hooked on a drug. Someone at the drop-in centre told me this was the place to come.'

'We get plenty of people like you, and we can always help them. You will have to try not to buy the drug – if you take it again, please let me know. It might take you a long time to recover. Do you have something which is bothering you that might have attracted you to drugs? Something which is always happening to you or that you are always thinking about, or that stresses you?'

'People revile me because I am Bajau. They blame me for dynamite fishing, which I have nothing to do with. I was nearly raped by a man who grabbed me from behind and I am frightened of it occurring again. I often think of my brother who died.'

'Those are good reasons for taking a drug. You need therapy. How does the drug make you feel?'

'Very happy. Like I was in Heaven with my brother. I feel things I have never felt before.'

'So the drug helped you?'

'It did mostly, but when it wore off, I felt lifeless and depressed. I suffered more because I craved to have it again. And it was costing too much. If I go on taking it, it will ruin my life.'

'So you neglected your health, eating and sleeping habits, and appearance and responsibilities.'

'I always did my duties for my family – selling the fish and buying the provisions every day.'

'I admire you for holding onto your feelings of obligation and disciplining yourself. I think you have the strength to work through giving up this addiction.'

Zoe put her down for group sessions and made another appointment.

Ayesha gave herself treats of food, like chocolate, when she was recovering. Everything felt new and clean and good now.

Remembering her taking the drug, Chris said, 'I remember how awful I felt when I had cancer. The treatment was a struggle I wouldn't want to go through again, I'd rather die.

'Somehow, from that I understand you and feel for you going through drug withdrawal.'

'The woman at recovery doesn't discriminate against Bajau people. I am not eligible for services, but she ignores it.'

'I think you will find that individual people feel that it isn't fair and act accordingly. They have professional standards about it.'

He had now worked his way up from odd jobs to being a handyman after the cyclone created a demand for house repair. He said he hoped to become a builder.

Princess Ayesha still hadn't completed the tale of her life. That night, she said, 'When my husband lay dying, I was devoted to his care. People came from far and near to say goodbye. They were his loyal and dedicated subjects. By then, our son had left home for his new life as head of the Bajau. As it turned out, after my husband's death the people wanted me to take up his position as ruler. I did this for many years – I knew the job well. I always consulted with knowledgeable people in making decisions about what to do in a matter. I had not sought this position in life but, when it fell to my lot, I felt I owed it as long as the people desired it.'

'You certainly achieved a great life,' said Ayesha, feeling a little tired out.

'You must achieve something in your life, Ayesha.'

'I intend to.'

CHAPTER 17

Sister Rosa had wanted the students to enact spontaneously a play about Jesus, which they had declined to do because no one was willing to play Jesus. But now the students decided to put on Romeo and Juliet as street theatre. They would do it when ready, in the park. The film of it was being shown in the local cinema just now, so people were familiar with the story. The snacks and souvenirs shop where the park adjoined the street would advertise it on their pavement billboard.

Jake and Tomasin were keen to play the parts of Romeo and Juliet. Gideon offered to play the priest, as his father had priestly clothes he could wear. Ayesha was to play the nurse, Noora volunteered to be the suitor Paris, Sunny would be Juliet's cousin Tybald and Hannah, Juliet's father. They would dress up in clothes which suited the parts and made them appear old-fashioned. The rest of the students were in the crowd, mingling with the audience.

At the start, everyone was at a ball, wearing masks. They danced around on the grass. The actors drew back into a circle as Jake and Tomasin gazed at each other adoringly and Jake kissed Tomasin's hand before they danced solo inside the circle.

A jihadist in the audience called out, 'We don't

approve of plays!'

Someone said, 'Oh, shut up. Why are you watching if you don't like it? Go away!'

All the players now took off their masks and blended with the audience. Tomasin stepped into the open circle again and called, 'Romeo, Romeo, where are you, Romeo? I love you.'

Jake came into the circle and said, 'I take you at your word. Call me but love.'

He raised his hand and looked questioningly at the audience. There were many wolf whistles.

Ayesha, as the nurse, standing behind Tomasin, said, 'Juliet, come in from the balcony. It's time for bed.' Tomasin turned and merged with the audience again.

Jake called, 'Good night, good night – parting is such sweet sorrow that I shall say goodnight until tomorrow.'

Gideon, the priest, walked into the space and said to Jake, 'You look as if you haven't slept all night.'

Jake said, 'It's true. I'm so in love with Juliet. I wish to marry her.'

All the students in the audience said, 'Ooh,' prolonging the sound, and others took it up.

Gideon said, 'So you will, and I'll perform the marriage today,' and he went back to the crowd.

Ayesha came forward again. Jake said, 'Tell Juliet to come to the priest's this afternoon for him to marry us.' Ayesha went to Tomasin and whispered in her ear.

Jake and Tomasin met up again in the playing space, and Gideon married them. He said to Romeo, 'Say after me, "I, Romeo, take you, Juliet, to be my wife",' and

Romeo repeated it. Turning to Juliet, Gideon said, 'Say "I, Juliet, take you, Romeo, to be my husband",' and she did the same. Gideon said, 'I pronounce you both man and wife.' Joining their hands, he said to Jake, 'You may kiss the bride.'

Jake embraced and kissed Tomasin. The audience cheered and clapped. Jake went on hugging and kissing Tomasin and she kissed him back. Some people in the audience kissed and hugged each other. Then others began to call out, 'Enough of it!' Tomasin and Gideon left.

Now Sunny stepped into the space with Jake. He said, 'I am Juliet's cousin, Tybald. I don't like the attention you're giving to Juliet. She's only fourteen.'

'He has married her,' a man in the audience said.

'Don't tell him,' another said to the man.

Sunny and Jake started to have a fight. Jake swung a punch at Sunny, and they acted at punching each other, with one or the other falling down from time to time. The audience cheered and egged them on. Some students yelled out 'Come on, Romeo, knock him out' and 'I'm backing Tybald to win'. At last, Sunny lay on the ground as if dead after a terrific swipe from Jake.

A policeman had appeared in the audience. He walked up and said to Jake, 'I am arresting you for assault,' and took out some handcuffs. Sunny jumped up quickly before the policeman could take his pulse, and Jake punched him down without contact so the policeman could see no one was getting hurt. Everyone clapped.

The policeman then said that they should have applied for a permit to act a play in the park. The audience booed him and someone said, 'We are all playing in the park together.' Some children agreed.

'Please don't shoot us, Mr Policeman,' a girl said.

'The police don't shoot children.'

'Well, that's a blessing at least,' her father said.

A very little boy held up his wrists close together and said, 'Arrest me.' The policeman laughed.

One of the students said to the policeman, 'Would you please tell Romeo that he's banished from this country for killing Tybald?'

'What?'

'Just say "I banish you, Romeo".'

The policeman shook his finger at Jake. 'I banish you, Romeo, never to return.' Everyone cheered him. Jake walked away.

But then, Jake returned with Tomasin. The audience gasped as the lovers embraced and lay down on the ground. 'One last pash all night,' said Jake.

Someone called, 'Don't get pregnant, Juliet.' They went on pashing.

'That's enough,' a person said. Jake got up and sneaked away.

In came Hannah dressed as Juliet's father, and said, 'Juliet, Paris is coming to marry you today.' The audience gasped again.

'She's already married,' said a woman.

'*Ssh, ssh,*' people said. 'You mustn't tell her father.'

'Noor is sick and can't play the part of Paris,' said Ayesha.

'I'll play it,' said a man standing nearby.

'No, *I'll* play it,' said Varsha, pushing herself through the crowd. 'You all forgot to contact me when you were choosing the players.'

'Oh, sorry,' said Ayesha softly, 'say loudly "I am Paris come to marry Juliet".'

So Varsha said it to Hannah.

But Tomasin had left the stage. When the others had gone, she came on with the priest, Gideon. She said, 'Paris is coming to marry me, but I'm already married to Romeo.'

'We understand that,' said someone in the audience.

Gideon said, 'I will give you a potion that will put you to sleep for a while so people will think you are dead.' He handed her the potion in a bottle, and she drank it. She lay down as if dead. 'Don't tell anyone she's really alive,' Gideon told the audience before going.

Ayesha the nurse said, 'We must tell Romeo that Juliet is not really dead before news reaches him that she *is* dead.' She looked for Jake but could not see him. Jake was having a pee behind a bush, where no one was in sight.

Hannah returned to the circle with Varsha as Paris. She said, 'Look, my daughter is dead.' They sat by the body and sobbed. Some young children in the crowd were crying and had to be comforted. Then Hannah and Paris left.

Jake came back, saw Tomasin was apparently dead, and drank from a bottle marked 'Poison'. The crowd were shouting, 'Don't kill yourself, Romeo', 'She's alive!', but he didn't believe it. He kissed her, saying, 'Thus with a kiss I die' and collapsed. Tomasin woke up. She saw Jake was lifeless. She kissed him, saying, 'His lips are still warm. I hope some poison is on them'. She seized his dagger from its sheath and stabbed herself through the heart. Many people screamed. It was a retractable trick dagger.

The students clapped to show the audience it was the end of the play, and they all applauded, shouting 'Bravo' and such things.

After the play was over, Ayesha was talking with Jihad near the jetty when she saw Omar coming along with a girl on his arm. She was wearing a headscarf. As they drew closer, she greeted them. The girl's name was Fauziah.

'We're just taking a stroll along the waterfront on a lovely evening,' Omar said.

'I've heard about you,' said Fauziah to Ayesha, 'and admire you for taking the literacy class. I'm a student at the Muslim girls' school.'

'She usually has a chaperone if she goes out with a boy,' said Omar. 'I've been allowed a privilege.'

'Is it so strict?' said Ayesha.

'Yes, my parents are like that towards young women too, and my grandparents even more so,' said Omar.

'The students at the boys' school throw stones and gravel from the schoolyard at girls in the street if they are not properly covered up – usually they are tourists,' said Fauziah.

'I've heard young men say, "You fuck" as they pass girls in the street that look like this, too,' said Omar. 'Tourists often behave badly in foreign countries because they don't care what people think when no one knows them.'

'That's all true,' said Jihad. 'Muslim people will say a girl is a prostitute if she's too free in her behaviour. Young women even need protection from men who might ordinarily behave well, but in crowded trains and buses, will feel—'

'I don't want to hear this,' said Fauziah.

'Sorry.'

'Those men would be of any religion, wouldn't they?' said Ayesha.

'Of course,' Omar said.

Fauziah continued, 'Many girls I know will marry when they leave school because their parents wish them to be safe and secure, but I want to continue my education so that I'm trained for a job.'

'So do I,' said Ayesha. Goodness, I didn't know all this before, she thought. I hope the Muslim state, where I can have free education, is set up soon.

'Will you have universities in your separate state?' she said to Omar.

'Yes.'

'Could women go there, and be treated equally?'

'Just so.'

No one would discriminate against me there, thought Ayesha.

'It will be a long time before you build and set up a university, if ever, won't it?' she said.

'It all takes a long time – we will build the mosque first,' said Omar. 'The Prophet Mohammad told us, "If you have a branch of a date palm in your hands and you know tomorrow is going to be the end of the world, plant it in the ground".'

CHAPTER 18

There seemed to be more than the usual flu going around. Then people heard of the pandemic. *It won't come here,* they thought. They were wrong. Ayesha didn't see Jihad at the beginning of it. Probably he was self-isolating at home. At the back of the drop-in centre, there were no longer drug dealers to be seen; police were clearing them off the street, even shooting them.

In the pandemic, there was an increase of homeless people who slept on the street at night because they had lost their jobs and could not afford to pay for accommodation. They were often beaten up, and had their bags snatched and their money stolen.

Sometimes, poor people stole a loaf of bread to stay alive. In Ayesha's eyes, this was okay because the Bible said it was. Sometimes, kind folk gave the starving food.

At a later time, sick people were falling down in the street, like drunks, dying in the gutters. Vultures pecked at the bodies. Ayesha thought of them dying and lying under the earth with worms and garden bugs eating holes in their bodies and in their orifices. It was like the Black Death she'd heard of.

An old street sweeper with a grey beard was sweeping the streets and gutters, his dreary, habitual task, raking up torn, dirty and blood-stained garments with other debris.

The street rubbish bins were overflowing. Ayesha saw a man spreadeagled on a park bench and wondered if he was drunk, very tired or dead. Ambulances eventually turned up to pick up bodies. They'd run out of plots to bury them in and were tipping them together in huge pits.

Looking at houses as she passed by, Ayesha saw writings on the walls and the faces of ghostly souls in the damp marks. They were the dead, denied their headstones, painting in shades of grey their own remembrance.

The drop-centre had closed its doors but was still being run by the staff who lived there, who were collecting, preparing and cooking food. People could queue in front of the centre along the pavement, and food and hot drinks in containers were passed to them from a window at mealtimes. If the food ran out, some people waited for the next meal sitting on the pavement and leaning on the centre wall, or others went away and risked their place in the queue for the meal.

Near the hospital entrance, people were congregating with their sick relatives, trying but failing to get them admitted to hospital. Armed guards stood at the doors to deny them entry. They said there was no room for more patients. The sick were sitting and lying everywhere on the concrete near the entrance. On rare occasions, medical staffers would come out with a stretcher and take a person in.

A hospital staffer came out of the doors to bring in another patient because someone had died and their bed was available. They checked around the sick and took the one in worst shape. They called orderlies for a stretcher.

There was a rumour going around that someone had invented the virus and was deliberately spreading it as a form of jihad.

In the street farther out, people were demonstrating, holding up placards which read 'No beds for sick people', 'Where are the medical supplies?', 'What are the doctors and nurses doing?', 'Safer to stay at home to die'. Some of the sick were not going to hospital in case they caught the virus there. From time to time, police came and cleared the demonstrators and people congregating.

A message reached all the students in Sister Rosa's class that she was in hospital in a bad way with the virus. They got together and arranged to go to her bedside with flowers on one day. They would have to wear face masks. The nurse had told Sister Rosa in advance that the students were coming to see her.

Arriving at the hospital, they were shown into Sister Rosa's room and were allowed to sit around the edge of it with their masses of flowers. One by one, each spoke a personal message to her. Sister Rosa was just lying still and couldn't speak, but she could hear them, the nurse said. After a while, she told them to leave. A few days later, they heard Sister Rosa had died. When they enquired if she had died from the pandemic virus, the hospital told them that it wasn't known because of their lack of testing kits. When an old person had more than one illness, they could have died from any or all of them.

After Sister Rosa's death, Ayesha went to the convent one day to enquire whether her class was starting up again, but a nun told her that no one was taking up Sister Rosa's classes for the remainder of the year. After the pandemic, they were putting on a complete secondary school class for adults she could enrol in, which would be more suitable for her. The class would run all day so that the students could proceed quicker than children in regular secondary school.

Ayesha met with Chris one day for coffee. He had a black eye.

He said, 'I ran into a thief who was stealing goods in the back of a shop. When I went to grab the parcels he was carrying, I was beaten up, and left.'

Ayesha said, 'Oh, the newspaper says the terrorists are shooting and bombing in the markets and on the buses and the police have so much to do they can't get around everything.

'There is more violence in homes with men beating and even killing their wives.'

'Well anyway, in this pandemic I keep accepting any kind of job, which is difficult to get at present. Just labouring, or anything. I'm still hoping to find permanent work in the construction industry.'

'As something to do in the future,' Ayesha said, 'I want to educate Bajau children, at least the young ones. If I can find someone to love and marry, and have children of my own, I'll teach them at home with the other children.

'I was taken in by things the students at the convent class said, as I didn't understand what they were talking about. They said I could go to university like them but, really I couldn't without secondary education. It was a fake world they presented to me, like the phantom things you see in windows. I was open to it because I didn't know.'

'Those students are still too young to understand many things,' said Chris. 'They like to sound more knowledgeable than they really are, and they make it up.'

She was surprised when he suddenly said, 'I want to say I love you, Ayesha. But even if you don't choose me, I'll always be your friend.'

Is he the one? thought Ayesha. She said, 'Oh. I'm not ready to marry yet, but I'll be your friend too. I'll never forget that you helped me to get off drugs. Actually, I think I'm now getting hooked on coffee! And it costs too much.'

'I drink too much coffee, too.'

Ayesha was relieved that they couldn't have a sexual relationship in the pandemic, as she didn't want that pressure.

She turned to walking the streets trying to find gardening jobs. She dropped in to Noor's place. She knocked on the door and then stood back to keep her distance. Noor opened the door and said she was the only one at home and to come in.

'We can sit far apart on the lounge chairs,' she said. 'What have you been doing?'

'I'm walking around looking for gardening work,' said Ayesha. 'I've never forgotten coming here and doing all that digging.'

'Are you finding many jobs?'

'No, but some. It all helps.'

'You are looking better now than when I saw you in the market that time. You were definitely unwell.'

'I was possessed by a Jinn, I thought, and had to keep it to save me. But eventually, I believed it was up to me to try and save myself. I'm fine now. Actually, I was on drugs. But I have gone through recovery at a special place. I was saved from getting worse by the pandemic, strange as it may seem.'

'I'm so glad for you, Ayesha.'

'That's okay. How is your mother?'

'She's always at the hospital tending to the patients. They need her working there as much as she can stand. I'm afraid she'll get the virus or just collapse from stress. But she won't take time off for a rest while there are people dying all around her. Dad has taken the opportunity to stay at home to write up his work and help support his family in these trying times. He's out shopping at the moment. The pandemic is a great leveller, don't you think?'

'If you mean it affects people equally, it doesn't. It's hurting the poor more.'

She ran into Sunny in the street. She almost didn't recognize him in his face mask. The clue was his red hair.

He said, 'Long time no see.'

'What are you doing these days?'

'Do you remember my report about the street children?'

'Yes.'

'There's even less room for them at the inn, so to speak, in these pandemic times. So I found a shelter for them in a disused factory. It has broken windows and the door doesn't lock. I have to stay there every night to mind and guard them. One of them sleep-walks. If any are sick, I take them to a doctor the next day. I've gone around houses asking for mattresses, bedclothes and clothing. Having heard about my project, people come with food, even toys.'

'Goodness, Sunny, what a job you've taken on. Is there anything I can do?'

'Can't think of anything at the moment, but I'll leave it to you.'

'Well, I could come and do gardening around your old factory, if you tell me where it is.'

Sunny told her where. 'I'll ask people for seeds for the garden.' It'll be like my own garden, she thought. Chris would lend me a spade.

A man with a beard who seemed to know Ayesha came up to her in the street, and said, 'The virus is divine retribution for the moral and intellectual decadence of the West.'

'And material decadence?'

'Yes. We are pleased about the economic damage that ensued. Now security services are distracted, we will carry out operations–'

'Killing? I've heard and seen it all before. By the way, we are not the West here.'

The man walked on.

'Aren't you going to say something against women?' Ayesha shouted.

She told Jihad that a jihadist had verbally attacked her in the street, and she'd like to go to another meeting of the jihadists to find out more about them and where they were at now. She would go dressed in a burka which would cover all her body except her eyes.

At the meeting, the leader said, 'Today, we are discussing the pandemic and how it affects us. The virus is divine retribution. God is punishing all of us for the wrongdoings of women against men, leading men into immoral practices. The virus won't affect Muslims, though. You are safe to attend church or our meetings. Wash your hands frequently, as we always do in the mosque.

'We will step up our attacks on the infidels and recruit more followers to our cause. They are trying to spread the virus to us. You must redouble your efforts to set up our Islamic country. Train in martyrdom for Allah's cause, shouldering together the duty of jihad.'

Ayesha crept away at the end, not speaking to anyone.

CHAPTER 19

After Ayesha landed in town one day, she found people had moved out into the street because of earth tremors. Earthquakes were prevalent in their country. Ayesha noticed new cracks in the walls of the old buildings.

When she saw Chris again, he said, 'My old aunt left the room she lives in yesterday and has gone walking along the main road out of town in order to find her relatives. She hopes to pass the time of the pandemic with my family, who live on a farm.'

'How do you know?' said Ayesha.

'She told her next-door neighbour. I do go to see her now and again, but I had no idea what she was thinking of doing. I have no work at present and would like to try and find her on the road and tell her to come back. She's more likely to catch the virus from other people on the road doing the same as her or take it to my family. Would you come with me?'

'Oh. I'll have to ask Ma if she can manage selling the fish and doing the shopping. It isn't so much now that Grump died.'

Ayesha returned to Chris's room the following day, saying that she could accompany him. They set off up the road wearing face masks and carrying bread and water.

As they neared the boundaries of the town, they

noticed they were becoming increasingly crowded and funnelled into the one main road by the many folk going back to their family farms.

One of them said, 'We might as well be out here if we're going to have an earthquake.'

People were closer together and not always wearing face masks. They carried bundles of clothes and belongings knocking at you from every side. When they reached the end of the pavement, they formed more of a line at the edge of the road to avoid traffic, spilling over into grassy verges where they could sit and rest for a moment. There were many elderly people and young children.

Chris and Ayesha were now trying to overtake people on the traffic side of the line. It was going to take time to find Auntie Claire, as she had a day's march on them. She would be walking slowly.

As it grew darker in the evening, many people looked for a grassy spot to lie down on for the night. Some were carrying on walking until they dropped. The ground was dotted with little fires where they were cooking or keeping warm.

Chris and Ayesha walked in darkness until they were too tired to continue. They lay on the ground looking up at the stars. He cuddled her back and later they turned over and she cuddled his. Ayesha told Chris that if she spent the night with only a single man in the house, the Bajau would consider her married, but it hardly applied here!

In the morning, they asked others around them who they would find to live with, and how far and why they were going.

'We were frightened of catching the virus in town,' said a woman. 'A town is too crowded.'

'We are now crowded on the road,' said Ayesha. But people said they had made up their minds individually, not realizing that many might do the same thing.

'We were short of food and running out of money to buy it,' said another woman.

'We were told to stay at home and that's what we're doing,' said another. 'There's not so much virus where our families live in the country.'

'I might die at home and I want to see my family again before I do,' said a man.

'I lost my job and couldn't afford to pay the rent any more,' said another man.

Many others who heard him concurred. People were drawn to one another because they were all affected by the pandemic. They asked Chris and Ayesha why they were going.

Chris said, 'If you meet an elderly woman called Claire walking slowly, please tell her her nephew Chris is searching for her to see if she's all right.'

Everyone took up their bundles and started to walk again. They were now hoping to find a service station where they could fill their water bottles, and maybe buy something to eat, even sweets.

Chris saw an old church. He said, 'Auntie Claire might have found somewhere to rest here out of the weather.'

He and Ayesha tried to open a door into the church,

but it was locked. 'We must try to enter every church,' said Chris.

Farther along the road, they found a ruined church. They explored the ruin, picking up their feet over broken masonry. There was plenty of evidence that people took shelter there and had left behind clothing and scraps of food. Rats were visible in cracks and crevices. Birds were nesting in the rafters below holes in the roof. But Auntie Claire was not there.

Ayesha said, 'Do you ever go to a church to pray?'

'No. Do you?'

'No. I don't have a custom of going to church.'

'I always refused to go to church, as a child, but I believed in God.'

'I believe in God.'

One evening, an argument broke out amongst the travellers. A woman started to say nasty things about the nurses in the hospital.

'The nurses are passing on the virus to patients. They want them to get sick.'

Others immediately stood up for the nurses. 'They are doing a marvellous job. We should applaud them.'

'They are getting the virus because of the work they do. It's not their fault.'

'They are going to work when they feel sick,' said the first woman, determined to blame someone for the calamity.

'If they stayed at home, there would be no nurses left to replace them. It's difficult. They risk their own lives to help the patients,' said someone defending the nurses.

'They should stay at home, like all people sick with flu. Many patients in the hospital should never have gone there, passing on infection to others,' said another person in support of the first woman.

At last, someone said there was no point in fighting about it. They didn't believe nurses had any malice towards other people. Grumbling, everyone settled down for the night.

The next day, the road started to climb, to narrow, to lose the verges and to go around hills. As yet, few people had reached their destinations. Police from the city had caught up with the crowds now risking their lives to traffic on corners they couldn't see around.

'It's too dangerous here,' the police shouted. 'Go home!'

'We *are* going home!' the people shouted back. 'That's exactly what we're doing!' ... 'It's too dangerous in the city!'

They were descending into the rich flat meadow country on the other side of the hills, where there were many small farms. People began to disappear into them at a faster rate.

Chris said, 'We are nearly at my home. Maybe Auntie Claire has got there.'

They walked in a front gate and up a long drive. As they got closer to the house, Chris's father and sister, working in the fields, saw them coming and waved with joy. They ran to greet and embrace them.

'Sorry about our muddy hands,' said his sister, as Chris introduced Ayesha.

Chris said, 'We walked all the way from town trying to find Auntie Claire, who we were told had set off to come here. She was trying to get away from the virus, but I was worried about her.'

'Well, she hasn't arrived yet. Come into the house to see Mum and have something to eat.'

Chris's dad said, 'We have plenty of food as the truckers who usually take our produce to market in town aren't working because of the virus.'

'Maybe I could do a job driving it there for you,' said Chris.

'I could dig and weed the garden,' said Ayesha.

When they reached the house, Chris's mum was waiting on the doorstep to welcome them in, as she had seen them from the kitchen window.

'Come and stay as long as you like,' she said.

Chris said, 'This is Ayesha. She is my girlfriend for as long as *she* likes.' Ayesha looked chuffed.

That evening, Chris and Ayesha went to sleep on the carpet beside a warm log fire.

Auntie Claire eventually turned up at the farm. She had walked off on a side road a long way before she realized she must have made a mistake. Some kind people had given her food and pointed her in the right direction. She was well, but very tired.

Chris decided to run a business of trucking his family's produce to town to sell by the side of the road. He sometimes prepacked boxes of fruit and vegetables to sell door-to-door. Ayesha wondered if Chris could involve her mother in the business. She would ask him about it.

Ayesha grew a flower garden outside Sunny's children's shelter in a disused factory. People often came and picked the flowers when she wasn't there, but she didn't mind; she liked sharing the flowers with them. They only picked a few flowers and left plenty behind, as if they cared about conserving them. In her heart, Ayesha dedicated the garden to Sister Rosa Ignatius who had given her students so much. Sister Rosa had devoted herself to Ayesha particularly.

Sunny told her he had seen Gideon. He had suffered from the virus badly and was only recovering slowly. The virus could damage your heart or lungs and the effects might be felt in some people for years. Gideon was very fatigued and had shortness of breath. I bet he will be writing a lot of letters to his girlfriend in Israel, thought Ayesha.

CHAPTER 20

It was a stormy day as Ayesha rowed to the shore, rain drops scattering over sea that was surging back and forth. The canoe was going up and down gently sloping hills. It made her laugh as she tilted forward and back. Nearer the shore, the waves formed a line of frothy cream as they curled over ever so slightly at the top, and then they spread out like a blanket over the strand.

After the market, Ayesha wandered into a deserted side-street beside the drop-in centre when she saw a pile of fruit that someone had tipped onto the pavement. So much garbage was left in the street these days. As she walked closer, she observed that a lot of the fruit was spoiled or rotten, but some was edible. She picked out an apple to munch on.

A young man with a face mask appeared suddenly and asked what she was doing.

She said, 'You can see what I'm doing.'

The apple dropped to the ground as he grabbed her hands and handcuffed them behind her. He poked a gun into her back.

With his other hand, he threw open a door into a building and said, 'Walk up the stairs. I'll shoot if you call out.'

When they reached the top of the stairs, he pushed her

into a room and felt in her pockets. He retrieved the money she'd earned at the market, before leaving and locking the door behind him.

The room was a vacated office. It was deadly quiet. It seems this is a business that has closed because of the pandemic, Ayesha thought. Most things, like furniture, had been removed. She sat down on the floor.

After a while, she heard noises like the young man was sitting in the corridor outside, guarding her. He cleared his throat and mumbled something. He was smoking – she could smell the smoke.

It was probably lunchtime when he unlocked the door and brought in a bowl of rice and a mug of water. He removed the handcuffs.

He said, 'Use the rubbish bin as a toilet, there's plenty of paper around.'

'What are you keeping me here for?'

'You will have to pay to get out.'

'I don't have any money.'

'You'll stay here until someone pays. Let me know their name and where to find them.'

'I don't know anyone who could pay.'

The man left the room again. Ayesha looked out the window and saw only walls of another building very close, with boarded-up windows. She tried to open the window. It was locked.

To escape, I'd have to smash the window and jump two stories onto concrete. I'll have to find something in the office that can be made into a sort of rope or take off all my clothes. I don't think I'll be able to do it. The man would hear it and come running.

In the evening, the man brought another meal. She noticed he was starting to grow a beard.

She said, 'Do you know someone called Jihad?' She thought she saw a flicker of recognition in his eyes.

'No. Can he pay?'

'No. He's a friend and a jihadist in training. He helped to kidnap a man. I thought you might know him.'

The guard shrugged.

'Are you in training? Learning some skills? Physical and mental?' Ayesha continued.

'No.'

'I don't believe you. What are you practising for?'

'I don't know yet.'

'What do I have to pay, anyway?'

'We'll tell that to the person we contact on your behalf.' He went away.

Ayesha slept on the floor that night. My family will be noticing my absence now, she thought. They'll be very upset. They'll probably contact the convent tomorrow.

Some days went by and nothing much happened. She believed Jihad might have informed his group of her daily movements and they thought it would be good for a young person to practise their kidnapping skills on her. She found paper and pens in the abandoned office and began to write down the story of Princess Ayesha. She was always meaning to do it sometime.

The man had emptied her 'toilet' after the first day and, keeping his distance, had taken her to a bathroom so that she could wash herself. Thinking about ways of escaping, she noticed the light and exhaust fan. *I could probably wrench it off and climb through the hole into the ceiling by standing on the vanity unit.*

Then the man called out, 'Are you finished?' and rattled the door handle. He had brought a meal. He was enduring the same boredom as she, sitting outside in the corridor with his gun.

He has not even told me what I have to pay. He still has to ask someone. Chris and the students will be concerned about my absence by now. They will contact my family and go to the police. It's a pity none of them knows Jihad.

When the man next brought her a meal, Ayesha asked him what he thought of people who steal. He didn't answer.

'Because your kidnapping me, is stealing, isn't it?'

'If you pay, you are free to go.'

'Then why won't you tell me what I have to pay?'

'I will tell you soon when I know.'

He doesn't even know. 'So, for now you are a thief. The law and all people say it's wrong to steal. Doesn't your religion say so?' *He knows it does.* 'Have you no religion?'

'I'm Muslim.'

'What does God say about stealing?'

The man left the room and locked the door.

Noor was trying to find Ayesha at the drop-in centre. They told her she hadn't been seen for two days, which was unusual. Noor also met Chris there. He said he was worried as Ayesha seemed to have disappeared. Then Noor went to the jetty and spoke with Odin and he said Ayesha's family were very upset because she hadn't come home as she always did. He took her to Ayesha's home to speak with her mother.

'I'll do everything I can to locate her. I'll go to the police and get the other students onto the job. I'll keep trying,' Noor said. She was not confident the police would do much about it.

On the way back to shore, Odin said, 'Ayesha often talks with a young man called Jihad who stands with his motorbike at the jetty hoping to get casual jobs. I have seen him there from time to time – not recently.'

Noor passed on all her information to the other students and asked them to search for Ayesha. No one knew Jihad's address. Hannah said she would join Noor to walk around all the places Ayesha frequented in a day. They could investigate the surroundings of these places. They both felt that the alley between the drop-in centre and other buildings was a suspicious place. They went there and called out Ayesha's name but heard nothing.

Ayesha heard a scuffle and the sound of voices outside her room. There was loud knocking on the door, and police broke in, holding onto the young man handcuffed behind his back.

'We believe you were kidnapped,' a policeman said.
'I was.'
'Are you Ayesha and are you okay? You friends informed us that you had disappeared.'

'I am Ayesha.'

'Is this the man who captured you?'

'It is.'

'Has he fed you and not harmed you in any way?'

'Yes.'

'She was flirting with me,' said the man.

'Lucky you!' said the policeman. 'So then you threatened her with a gun and locked her up. We'll see if the gun's registered.'

'I was not flirting, liar. I didn't even speak to you,' Ayesha told the man. Turning to the policemen she said, 'They are against everyone who is not in their group. They hate women and see them as seducers of men, whereas regular Muslims are the opposite. They think women are purer than men, and it's men who have evil thoughts.'

'Regardless of your and his beliefs,' a policeman said, 'it's against the law to kidnap people and hold them against their will. You will both have to come to the police station with us.'

Chris had won a prize from a shop he went to frequently and he gave the ticket for it to Ayesha. It was for a visit to a spa. Chris said he didn't have time to go there and didn't want to anyway. It was more something she would like.

Ayesha presented herself at the spa to find out what she could have. She could have hairstyling, make up, manicure, and hot tub soak and scrub followed by massage.

'Can I have the hot tub one today, and the hairstyling and so on another day if I have a special occasion?' She had an idea in mind.

'Yes.'

So she had a wonderful relaxing time at the spa.

CHAPTER 21

The pandemic was almost over, but adults were still wearing face masks. Walking along the street, Ayesha saw a notice saying that well people could come to a nursery school on a particular day to observe how the children were taught. She met up by chance with Varsha there, who was interested in the same thing. They had both been attracted by the sign, which had only just been put up.

Varsha said, 'I'm thinking of becoming a teacher like my mother. But I don't know what age I want to teach yet.'

'I would actually like to be a nursery school teacher,' Ayesha said. 'I want to teach the Bajau children.'

They watched as the children did finger-painting and got paint on their clothes.

'It washes off easily,' said the teacher.

Later, she sang songs with them as she played on the piano. The children had drums, tambourines, cymbals, triangles and rattles to play. The children danced to dances they knew well, while singing too.

They sang a song with the teacher that went 'If you're happy and you know it, clap your hands', and clapped their hands. Ayesha and Varsha joined in.

'I like that song, said Ayesha. 'Singing it would *make* you happy.'

She asked a little girl, 'What do you want to be when

you grow up?'

The girl answered, "I want to be a robot.'

Everyone sat on the floor while the teacher read them a story, showing them pictures in the book. At last, the children went out to play on the swings and in the sandpit. The teacher explained to the visitors the many things she did, and why. She answered their questions.

Varsha said to Ayesha afterwards, 'Would you like to visit a primary school where my mother now teaches English as a second language? I've done it. We can sit and observe in the back of the room.'

'Yes.'

They arranged to go another time to do that.

Ayesha was again looking for work she could do. She found out about an escort agency for Muslims and went there.

When she was interviewed, the woman said, 'What is your age?'

'Sixteen.'

'That's okay. Do you have a birth certificate?'

'No, but I'll apply for it.' I'll never get one, she thought.

'That will do. You must be at least sixteen because it is the age of consent.'

'What is that?'

'It means it is legal for a man to have sex with you.'

'I don't want to have sex.'

'You don't have to have sex without your consent. An escort is not the same as a prostitute as there is no understanding you are there for sex, but the man may ask for it.'

'What would I say?'

'You could say that you will try to sexually please him without having sex.'

'How would I do that?'

'The man will tell you when you agree to go to a hotel room with him. You would meet him in a bar first.'

'I don't drink alcohol.'

'That's all right, you can have a soft drink. He will pay for it. Can you manage to hold a conversation with a strange man – discuss something of mutual interest, like hobbies, current affairs, school subjects, personal relations?'

'I'm not up in school subjects.' I had better not talk about the parables of Jesus, she thought. 'For personal relations, I have a non-sexual boyfriend.'

'This is not very promising. Don't mention your boyfriend. Did you know we are also a marriage service?'

'No. You help people find marriage partners?'

'Yes. Sometimes they find them when working as an escort. We have a list of people who want to meet someone to marry and try to match them, but we don't do the arranged marriages that some parents ask for. So we have two separate businesses. The Christians do them differently – escorts only or relationships only.'

'Why?'

'You do ask a lot of questions. Because there are only a small number of Muslims, we need to run them as two part-time businesses to make enough money.'

'I would like to do that.'

'Yes, but you would need training and experience first.'

'Well, actually I don't want to find another partner, but I could do escort in the day if I'm paid.'

'It would be harder to find work for you in the day, but you would be paid a small fee. Have you got some better clothes than jeans, t-shirt and trainers?'

'I have a good outfit with a skirt my mother made, and court shoes.' Mum had saved up and bought an old hand-operated sewing machine.

Ayesha was still owed hairstyling, makeup and manicure at the spa. She went along before her date. She had never before looked like what she ended up with. She had nails painted deep pink, a short, wavy hair style with dyed streaks to match her nails, lipstick, eye shadow and mascara, and false eye lashes. She looked like a film star.

When she arrived at the bar at the appointed time, she met her man there displaying a red handkerchief in the pocket of his jacket, as she'd been told he would. He was an older man, well-dressed.

Ayesha said, 'I am your escort.'

He said, 'I am pleased to meet you,' and shook her hand. 'What would you like to drink?'

'Just lemonade, please.'

He flicked his hand at the bartender, and said, 'That's what I'm drinking.' Possibly not, she thought.

After she'd had a sip, the man said, 'What has brought you here today?'

'I need to earn some money to help my family. Things have been not so good because of the pandemic.'

'You are a beautiful girl and very young.'

'I'm not practised in the ways of the world.'

'I like innocence. I would look after you. What are your hopes and dreams?'

'I want to be better educated and trained for a job, and I'm hoping to meet a nice man to marry and have a family with. What do you desire of me?' He's probably done it all, she thought.

The man sighed. 'Many things. But only small steps at first with you.'

Music had started playing, and the man indicated there was a dance floor. 'Would you like to dance?'

'Yes, but I've never learnt it.'

'I'll show you some steps.'

Soon she was dancing with him and enjoying it. This is not social distancing, she thought. Has everyone forgotten about it? After a while, they sat down at a little table away from the bar.

'Just relax,' said the man. 'Please excuse me while I go to the bathroom.'

While he was away, Ayesha thought he might be phoning his wife or girlfriend. She looked around the room and the bartender winked at her. I bet he gets a lot of practise in winking. The man returned and sat down again.

He said, 'I'll tell you about myself. I'm married but my wife is not so keen on me any more. She's happy with her life though and I don't want to upset her or the children. In the long run, I might find someone else to marry, but for now I've been seeking pleasure with other women.'

'How many other women?' said Ayesha, thinking of the concubines of the princess's husband.

'Just meeting them and seeing how it goes.'

'Oh yes, I see. The woman at the agency told me they do escort and also helping people find partners.'

'I'm looking at escorts first. I don't want to meet masses of them. I might find I'm happy to return to the same one.'

'I understand.'

'So, would you come with me to a hotel room? Of course, you will be paid for coming to the bar. It's your choice.'

'I don't think I will come to the hotel room.'

The man got up and politely escorted her to the exit door and said goodbye. I wonder if I could go on doing this, she thought. He's probably slowly collecting women whom he does things with in a hotel.

She was glad to be out of the gloomy light of the bar and into the blinding sunshine.

When she arrived home in the evening, Ma said, 'What has happened to your hair and face?'

Ayesha said, 'It will all wash out eventually.'

When Dad came home, he said, 'Where did you go looking like that?'

She said, 'I had a lunch date with a nice man.'

'Watch out for him with your uppity ways.'

'I didn't like him and am not seeing him again.'

CHAPTER 22

The sea was in a weird, disturbed state. Paddling to the shore, Ayesha found herself being pushed around in circles. There were whirlpools in the water. It was high tide. As she neared the shore, she saw all the trash that was there had been sucked into the whirlpools and was going round and round and down. It was like the Sargasso Sea that she'd heard of! It was doing a cleaning job, she imagined.

At lunch, she spotted Noor outside the drop-in centre.

'I came here to find you,' Noor said. 'Tomasin wants to hold a meeting to organize a 'Black Lives Matter' street march. It's in support of a similar march in America. Would you come to the meeting with me?'

'Of course, I will. But what is it about?'

'Well, in this country, people are not really black or white, as in America. They're different shades of brown. But what it means is that a group of people are discriminated against.'

'Like the Bajau.'

'Yes, and Muslims are discriminated against by the Christian majority.'

'The poor are suffering badly here in the pandemic and the police are hard on them.'

'You are right. We will band together to march along

the street and make speeches in protest against the discrimination and prejudice.'

Noor arranged to meet Ayesha outside the drop-in centre on the day of the meeting, and they would go together to Tomasin's place.

At the meeting, Ayesha saw that nearly all the crowd were from their class at the convent, milling around and getting acquainted again, as self-isolation had become relaxed. After a while, Tomasin tapped on a glass to start the meeting.

'You know I'm American. I've brought you here to discuss holding something like a 'Black Lives Matter' march and demonstration. It would have to be appropriate for this town. Which groups are discriminated against? We need to rope in more people with ideas of what the march should be about, and who should be in it. So far, those in our class have suggested the Bajau, Muslims and the poor.'

'Nurses and doctors in the pandemic,' said Hannah. 'They've been attacked and criticized for passing on the virus! Instead, we owe them a big thank-you.'

'The disabled,' said Varsha.

'Women have been more affected by the pandemic and the recession,' said Noor, 'because they have more of the jobs in childcare, health, hospitality and retail and leisure work, where more jobs have been lost now.'

'Factory workers have particularly lost jobs,' someone said.

'*Phew,* that's a lot,' said Tomasin. 'We should contact people in all the groups mentioned to join the march. I'll be getting permission for the march to take place, hopefully!'

'I was going to add,' said Jake, 'the police will be out seeing that the march is peaceful. But the police are particularly guilty of discrimination against some groups of people and we will probably have placards saying that. We need to make sure all our actions are peaceful.'

'If any violence breaks out, we can use passive resistance by sitting on the ground,' said Sunny, 'but some might get arrested because we would be blocking the road.'

'The march will end in the park where we can sit on the ground to listen to the people giving speeches,' explained Tomasin. 'If we can get there without trouble, perhaps hiding any placards criticizing the police till then, it would be best.

'So, everyone, please contact any groups you think appropriate and encourage them to join the march and make speeches. Invite them to the next and final meeting at my place.' She named a date.

By the time of the meeting, the 'All Lives Matter' group had grown to represent animals, plants, the ocean, the lgbtqiap community and victims of male violence. Therefore, everyone agreed to march under the banner of their group, such as 'All Plants Matter', and so on. It became the 'All Living Things Matter' march, which covered the environment groups. They were all to bring as many people to march as possible, including children, the elderly and people in wheelchairs.

Tomasin had obtained permission for the march to take place in a quiet and orderly manner along the main street and ending at the park, on a Sunday. They would wear face masks as a precaution and to set an example.

On the day of the march, the participants turned up as they had promised. A few police were posted along the side of the street. As it was Sunday, not many people were out and about and everything was very peaceful. The groups of onlookers grew as the marchers reached the park; a few people called out remarks and jeered. Reporters from the press and TV asked questions, took notes and made videos. A larger crowd built up as the speeches began but fell away again later in the day. There was no food and drink to be had in the park. The organisers of the march counted it a success.

When Ayesha was in the park on that Sunday, she noticed there were people standing on boxes addressing a small crowd on a subject of interest to them. It stayed in her mind, and she asked Ma if she knew about it. Ma said yes, and you were free to go there and give talks about anything you liked to the folk who strolled about, who often engaged in discussions with the speaker.

Ayesha thought she might talk in the park about the life of Jesus. The parables, or the miracles, would be too hard. She wasn't qualified to do it. But she could be like a news reporter and was prepared to discuss what Jesus' life had been like. She would want to do this because she admired him. She was like a fan. In the pandemic or the aftermath, people needed to feel inspired by Jesus.

She was nervous when she took to her stand in the park on a box she'd got from the market, clutching some notes she'd written. As she started speaking, some people paused to listen for a while, before moving on.

At one point, a man said, 'You're a Bajau girl, aren't you? I didn't think you people were Christians.'

'Jesus did good things and I can admire him even though I'm a Muslim. It's worth knowing about him and reading the Bible to see what he said and did.'

'That's very true,' said a woman, 'and many don't read the Bible.'

Another said, 'Come back and talk about Jesus again. People need it. They don't go to church.'

After this experience, Ayesha grew in confidence and made a habit of speaking in the park on Sundays. She talked about different religions. A man came up to her as she was giving a talk in the park one Sunday.

He said, 'I see you are good at making speeches. Would you say something about dynamite fishing and how destructive it is?'

'You ask me that when someone let off a bomb so close to our house that it shook? No one in my neighbourhood group does dynamite fishing.'

'I wasn't involved in that and I don't approve of it. I'm not trying to blame the Bajau any more, but I now see it's a question of poor people who are trying to make a living at what they normally do. Unfortunately, there's still the problem of depleting the fish and other creatures in the ocean, not to mention the plants.'

'Then what can the poor people do?'

'The government would have to fork out money to set them up in a new way of life. But till that happens, we must go on talking about it. Do you know about cyanide fishing too?'

'No.'

'You can spray a poison, cyanide, on the fish's habitat to stun the fish and catch it easily. But this method hurts or kills coral reefs. Corals feed and house sea creatures. Also, there is coral mining for making bricks, cement or any type of construction material; for medical purposes, marine aquariums, calcium and phosphate. Then there is bottom trawling–'

'Look, I'll make notes about it all and fit it in to what Jesus said in his parables.'

'What did he say?'

'He said that the world is a treasure which was given to us by God. No one owns any part of it nor are they free to harm it, but we are the stewards and caretakers of it.'

She wrote a speech which she gave in the park from her box to anyone who would listen:

'I want to ask you not to use destructive methods of catching fish, like dynamite or cyanide fishing, so that you are reducing the number of fish in the ocean. Eventually, there will be no fish left to eat, and poor people will no longer be able to catch fish for free.

'The fish was the sacred symbol of Christians. Jesus meant us to live in a world where there were always fish when he told his disciples to go out and be fishers of people. He said that the kingdom of Heaven was like a net that caught all kinds of fish. If there were no fish in the world, people would wonder what Christ was talking about and it would diminish the meaning of what he said.'

Ayesha thought she would write a speech about the

poor because they had not participated in the march as a group. Why? Someone has made them feel ashamed and guilty about being poor, she thought. The Bajau did not come too.

In the sermon on the mount, Jesus had said, 'Blessed are you that are poor'. Then Ayesha remembered he had also said, 'Blessed are you when people hate you and when they exclude you and revile you and spurn your name as evil'. So God stood up for people who, like her, were reviled and excluded. That would be the poor too. The people who did it were supposed to be Christians. She wrote that Jesus said too, if you hold a party, invite the poor and disabled who would not have the money to bring food and drink. Sell what you have and give the return to the poor, for you will have treasure in Heaven. She made this speech in the park. She went on repeating the speeches and writing new ones.

CHAPTER 23

Quite early one morning, Ayesha was paddling her canoe to the shore when she saw a boat coming directly towards her. She paddled faster to get out of the way in case it collided with the canoe. But it was a motorboat and kept coming in her direction as if the people in it, that she could now see more clearly, wanted to mow her down. The next time she glanced at it, she saw that it was too late and the men in the boat had rifles. At first, she thought they were officials who had to monitor shipping in case it was breaking the rules. They were wearing some sort of uniform. She remained calm as a man took hold of a side of the canoe.

'You are coming with us.'

'What have I done wrong? I always go this way every day.'

The man stayed silent and manhandled her onto the boat. They also took on board her catch of fish. Someone hit the accelerator.

'Look, my canoe is drifting away.'

'Never mind. Sit here, be quiet and don't move.'

'What are you doing?'

'We are removing you to be in our group.'

'I don't want to be in your group.'

'You have no choice. We will not harm you.'

'How come you picked me?'

The man shrugged. After this, the men took no notice of her if she spoke. She had a strong urge to dive into the water and swim to her canoe, now disappearing into the distance. But if she did, they might shoot her.

Shortly, she said, 'Where are we going?'

'You'll be told when it matters. You will be safe.'

An interminable time passed. Ayesha watched the water slip by in an almost hypnotic state. It was hopeless. The men had probably abducted her for money. Her family would have nothing to pay with. No one would help them. Everyone was poor these days.

The people at the convent school would try to help her! That was her only hope. Someone would rescue her.

She looked around the boat for food. Apparently, there was none. Then one of the men took a loaf of bread out of a bag and passed it around to the others, who broke off chunks. When they had finished, the man in charge of the bread took off a piece and handed it to her. A bottle of water was passed on and she and the others had a drink from it.

The day continued without event. They were skirting the coast. Every now and then, some people on boats waved or shouted. There was no way Ayesha could attract their attention. The only time one of the men spoke to her was to say, 'We are going to an island.'

Towards evening, Ayesha could see what appeared to be an island looming up. She saw dense forest, with mountains, coming ever closer. Soon they were in the shade of a steep mountain near the shore. The water was choppier.

They had a bumpy ride into a small beach. The boat driver cut the engine. The boat came to a stop in the sand. Everyone jumped out.

'You can come out of the boat now, but if you run away, we will shoot you.'

How could I run away into the jungle? thought Ayesha. Without food, I would not survive. She was feeling hungry again.

'We have a long march ahead of us,' said one of the men.

Ayesha had on her usual t-shirt, jeans and trainers. My shoes will carry me safely along, she reckoned. My legs are protected from prickly vegetation.

Just beyond the narrow beach, there were mangroves before the slope of the mountain started. Soon she was stumbling through the mangroves, her shoes immersed in water and tree branches smacking against her upper body as she tried to protect her face with her hands.

The mangroves came to an end, and everyone began to follow a narrow path up the mountain. It went on and on. Huge trees soared above them. They halted for a rest now and again, and to drink some water.

A man explained, 'We are trying to reach our camp by nightfall, so we can't rest for long.'

They allowed her to piss behind a tree. Overhead, the canopy was so thick that she couldn't see the sun. It was dark. She could hear the birds of the forest far above. She had to pull off leeches attaching themselves to any flesh they could find.

She went on wearily plodding up the path. It wound around rocks, and over roots that she almost tripped on. Once she tripped and bumped her knee. The man behind pushed her up roughly with the butt of his rifle. She was so tired. She felt she was running out of legs.

They reached a downward turn in the path almost at the top of the mountain. There was no view to be had because of trees. From then on, it was downhill, sometimes steep. She kept walking, almost falling, frightened of the slope, like a zombie. She lost her sense of time. It was getting darker.

At last, they arrived at the camp. It was very dark here. She was locked into a small hut made of sticks. She could only just stand straight up in it.

The guard said, 'We are close to a river and will bring water.'

No water came to her. She had to lie on the ground save for some large leaves spread on it. She had no covering but her clothes. It was cooler at night in this hill country than what she was used to. Shivering, she rolled herself into a ball and hugged herself to sleep.

When it seemed to be morning, she waited for food, stuffing her fists into her mouth with hunger. Breakfast came, a bowl of rice soup. It was edible. It partly assuaged her thirst. Only just in time, a guard took her outside to go to the toilet behind a tree. There was a bush toilet but Ayesha was in a rush. The guard gave her a roll of toilet paper to keep.

She said, 'I need more water to drink.'

He said, 'If I don't give you too much, you won't have

to pee so much.'

She was allowed to have a shower from a hose attached to a pump in the river. She kept her clothes on, as the guard didn't leave, and drank more water from it. He turned off the hose and departed to get her fresh clothes; a pair of black pyjama pants and a pink t-shirt. He turned his back for her to undress and put on the dry clothes. Ayesha was all the while anticipating he would turn around and look at her, but he didn't. Not this time maybe.

Another man came and said, 'You probably know you have been kidnapped for a ransom. The sum you must pay us for your freedom is one million dollars. If you don't pay within a certain time, we will kill you.'

'I don't have such money. Why would you kidnap me? My family is poor. I don't know where they could get it from. How much time do I have?'

'We will let you know later. We could kill you any time. Someone will take a message to your parents.'

'I'm only a child.'

'It doesn't matter to us.'

She was locked in the hut again. Nobody to talk with. She would have to endure sitting in this tiny space all day with nothing to do. She constantly thought about her life. She wondered what her parents were doing after discovering she had disappeared. Perhaps they had found the empty canoe. They might be worried that she had drowned. But they knew how well she could swim.

It would take a while for them to think of going to the police because of the way people treated the Bajau. Before that, they would search the ocean round about. They would go to the convent and tell the nuns. Gideon would know of her absence by now, and *he* would go to the police, and try to think of something he could do. People would advise him. Gideon would do anything for her. And Chris would too.

What of Jihad – was he somehow linked to this business? He had shown interest in these radical groups and was always looking for ways of making money. But he was a 'do nothing' person. He would say people ought to do such-and-such but do nothing himself.

Ayesha found herself being bitten by mosquitoes. She was constantly slapping them as they landed on her. She would ask the guard when she saw him next if there was anything you could do about them. She could see out of the hut, through the gaps between the sticks, the guard sitting a short distance away, smoking. She felt the walls and ceiling of the hut – the same sticks were on the ceiling – but it was very firmly put together with chicken wire on the outside. No escape. She realized now, if it rained, she would always get wet.

If these men are truly Muslim, they might have some sympathy for me for being of similar faith. I will listen to see if they pray at times during the day. I must pray too.

At dinner time – early – the guard brought a small meal of rice and a mug of water. It was little indeed. Later, Ayesha heard voices of the men at prayers.

She remembered Princess Ayesha and having conversations with her. She was left clinging to a tree in a storm, not knowing if anyone would save her. She might have let go and drowned, or starved to death, when no one came. I must hang on, thought Ayesha, and not give up because of despair.

CHAPTER 24

After a few days, Ayesha was startled to hear sounds like captives arriving at the camp. The door of the hut suddenly opened, and a man and a woman were pushed into the hut. The door was locked behind them.

Ayesha jumped up from where she was sitting. 'Who are you? Are you all right?'

'Yes,' said the man. He helped the woman to the ground and sat down. They looked tired out. They were young. Ayesha sat down again.

She said, 'I've been here a few days, I think. Perhaps longer.'

The woman said, 'I'm very thirsty.' She had a foreign accent.

Like Ayesha, the couple only had with them the clothes they were wearing.

Ayesha said, 'It's cold at night here, but there is plenty of fresh air.'

The man said, 'When do we get fed?'

'We only get two meals a day. They may bring one soon.'

'What about washing and washing clothes,' said the woman. She looked as though it was an effort to speak. She had wanted a drink. She began to cough.

The man made her lie down. He lay beside her and put

his arms around her. 'We'll just lie here quietly, not speaking.'

Ayesha thought, the couple will roll away from each other as they get too hot. There will be just enough room for the three of us to lie side by side at night. I'll ask if I can sleep on one side of the hut, with the woman beside me. She started to scrape leaves over to her side.

Later, it was mealtime again. A plate of rice with some horrid-looking pieces of meat in it to share between three people, and a mug of water each. The couple introduced themselves as Ove and Solange.

Solange did not seem well. She was very drowsy but she managed to eat. Ayesha asked Ove how they were captured. He said they were on holiday at an almost deserted beach when two men arrived in a car. They parked near the couple and asked them the way to the nearest town. They said they had a map in the car so the couple walked over to point out their position on the map. All at once the men drew guns and forced them into the car. They sped along the road to where they met up with another man waiting in a boat. The three men brought them to the island.

'Have you heard of this separatist group?' said Ayesha.

'Yes.'

'They are Muslims. I am Muslim too. I'm going to discuss it with them. I have told them I have no money for a ransom. I stand to be killed, but possibly they'll spare me because I am Muslim.'

'You could try. We're not Muslims. We are young

and also don't have money. You'd think they'd try to capture rich people.'

'Probably they do. They think any tourist is rich.'

The guard came to let them out to use the bush as a toilet. Ove had to assist his wife to walk there, she was so floppy with exhaustion.

The guard said, 'No washing till tomorrow.'

They managed to sleep all together in the hut. It was more humid with three people and the mosquitoes were bad.

Lying awake. Ayesha wondered whether Jihad knew any of these particular jihadists. He had gone to their meetings and had worked with some of them to kidnap and lock up people in town. He always needed money. She hadn't seen him for a while.

Suppose Jihad had told them about her, how she rowed a canoe on her own from the stilt houses to the jetty early in the morning, a perfect time to abduct her – that was it! How else would they have chosen her. Jihad might be somewhere in the camp. She would ask the guard in the morning.

Ayesha was woken up at dawn by the sound of someone being sick. She recalled she had heard cries when she was half awake. Solange had called the guard to let her out to vomit on the ground outside the hut. Ayesha felt queasy herself; it might have been from the meat they ate. She told the guard the next time he came that the meat they ate was bad.

He said, 'If you complain about the food, I will make you eat your own shit.'

There was the usual routine of breakfast and going out to wash. Ayesha asked the guard if he knew someone called Jihad in his group. He said no, but he seemed surprised by the question and then looked away furtively. I bet he's lying, she reckoned.

She noticed she wasn't getting her periods any more. She knew she wasn't pregnant. She told Solange about it.

'Oh, it's because of the stress you're experiencing in these hard conditions,' she said. 'The periods will come back when you get home again.'

In the night, Ayesha had a dream. She swam down to where Dido died, and there was a terrible darkness. Ancestral voices from Hell told her not to go there. She was to leave before worse happened and was not to look back when leaving. She turned for home but cast her eyes back to see the spot where Dido was last alive. A groan went up which meant she would die before her time, like Dido. When she woke up, she felt weighed down by this awful prediction.

Ayesha was surprised by Jihad showing up at the door of the hut.

'Well, I thought you might be here,' said Ayesha.

'I joined the group. I like working with them. I'm desperate for money.'

'They have threatened to kill me if I don't pay one million dollars.'

'They won't. I won't let them. You are my friend. I'll tell them it's true your family couldn't pay.'

'I think they captured me because you talked about me.'

'I'm sorry.'

'Are any of Omar's group here?'

'No. Ayesha, I won't let anything happen to you. I have to live in the same conditions as you.'

'Tell them I'm a Muslim too.'

'Okay. You'll hear from me again soon.'

The inhabitants of the hut went on feeling sick or being sick from the meat. They thought it was something disgusting like the intestines of an animal. They were getting thinner.

The guard was trying to look at Ayesha when she took off her clothes to wash.

She said, 'If you do that, I will throw dirt in your eyes.' Yes, that's what I'll do now! She bent down, picked up a handful of dirt and threw it in his eyes.

'I'll shoot you.'

'Rubbish.'

Ayesha surprised herself, but he was like a child being naughty.

'Turn your back,' she said. That's what he usually did. She proceeded to undress.

Suddenly, he turned around and saw her stark naked. She grabbed the clothes and covered herself.

'That's a payback,' said the guard, with a smirk.

As Ayesha was going to sleep that night, the princess made herself known again. She said, 'My son, when he was little, strayed into the forest to play without anyone noticing it. When we did, we went out calling for him. People came from near and far to search in the forest, and a whole night passed before he was found. He was happily playing in a tree. He said that the monkeys brought him fruit and nuts to eat.

'He chirped proudly, "I stayed in the forest on my own!"'

Chris did not see Ayesha at the drop-in centre for days on end. He asked people about her but heard nothing. He spoke to Odin at the jetty and he said she hadn't been coming back and forth in her canoe. He went to the convent and they said she had disappeared. At the police station, they thought she might have been kidnapped by the separatists for a ransom. They often set up camps in the coastal islands. Chris decided to hire a motorboat and search for Ayesha around the islands. He would drive the boat around every one of them and examine all the coastlines. Admittedly, this wasn't much, but he felt her captors would have visible landing places.

Chris set off in the boat and spent a considerable time driving around the islands. He drew rough maps of where there were landings or beaches. If he saw, from a distance, people on a shore, he would go in for a closer look.

Jihad came back in the dead of night. Ayesha heard a quiet scratching at the base of the hut. Then, 'It's Jihad, it's Jihad' in a whisper.

'What?'

'I'm ready to go. The guard is asleep.'

She already had her shoes on and stole out the narrow opening of the doorway. Jihad took her hand. He guided through bushes in a little path he had cased out.

When they were some distance away, he whispered, 'I thought about it long and hard and I changed my mind. As your friend, I can't let you die! I have some food in my knapsack. We'll have to find water as we travel – it rains often.'

Much farther on, he said, 'We can't take the track we came in on. We'll have to walk through the forest.'

He had a large sharp knife, in a bamboo sheath, for cutting their way through it. They had no compass and would not be able to pinpoint distant objects to walk towards. They would hardly know day from night.

CHAPTER 25

They began to walk through the jungle. They tripped over tree roots as they felt their way with their arms. Long vines slapped them in the face. Ayesha started to feel her face and bare arms, stinging. She was constantly pulling off leeches. Jihad always walked in front and used his knife to slash the undergrowth.

He turned around and said quietly, 'This will take a long time.'

'Sometimes people go on a "long walk",' Ayesha said wryly.

In the morning, faintly recognizable, they ate some bread that Jihad brought. They went to the toilet behind shrubs and tree trunks. Ayesha saw a snake when she was squatting and held her breath, hoping, if it bit her on the bottom, that it wasn't poisonous. She managed to jump up in time. She'd heard that snakes kill more people than car accidents do.

They set off, slashing and trudging for hours. When night fell, hardly noticeably, they ate the last of their food. Jihad decided to clear a space for them to sleep in a more open place. They threw themselves down, exhausted. They did not feel creepy crawly things that bit them in the night.

They would have to find food in the forest every day now. The bites on their faces were swelling into lumps.

'It looks like nothing actually poisonous bit us yet,' Ayesha observed in the morning.

This day, the forest opened up to a farm, but the fugitives felt they couldn't risk contacting the farmer in case he was a supporter of the militants. They crawled, under the cover of a crop, until they found vegetables to eat raw. They decided to keep to the edges of farms if they came across more of them. This lasted a few days, but then the jungle loomed up.

They trekked again through the jungle vegetation, up and down hills and mountains. Sometimes, they heard a helicopter overhead. They ate various bugs and plants that they found.

'In ancient times,' said Ayesha, 'people must have had to try eating anything. Sometimes, they died from it.'

They came to a dirt road and decided to cross it so as to keep away from all human traffic in case it was unfriendly. It would be better to reach the coast. They found themselves in a huge plantation of coconuts. They stayed for a few days living off coconuts, which Jihad opened with a slash from his knife, cutting his fingers a little. They drank the milk. One time, they encountered a snake, which Jihad tried to kill with his knife, but it got away.

'We should kill a snake to eat,' he said. 'It might be venomous, but not if you cut off its head.'

'It would be dangerous to catch them.'

After a spell of walking through the jungle again, they crossed a road into a rubber plantation. It seemed to go on forever. They observed the coolies make a 'v' slash on the tree and attach a cup under it to collect the sap that trickled down. They paid no attention to Ayesha and Jihad as if they were used to seeing strangers wandering over the plantation. It was a pleasant change to walk through the rubber trees. They learnt to catch insects and worms to eat, and could find pools of water to drink from, with small bugs swimming in them.

When they returned to the forest, Ayesha thought of the spirit people she believed in; the spirit of the water, of the mountain, of the trees. They came across a magnificent waterfall with a rainbow playing on the mist it sent up. They managed to walk along a rock ledge behind the fall and wash in it, laughing with excitement and danger. For Ayesha, it was a world that was familiar, inspiring and beautiful. Jihad said he had never thought about it.

'What is beauty?' he said.

'It is what you like; it is art.'

Every morning, and in the evening if they weren't too tired, Ayesha prayed with Jihad by kneeling towards the east and chanting prayers as she bent down to the ground and up again.

Jihad said in prayer, 'O Allah! Bless the food you have provided us and save us from the punishment of hellfire.'

How apt that is in our circumstances, thought Ayesha.

The forest thinned out and Ayesha and Jihad burst through some trees, and there, unexpectedly, was the sea. They ran to the beach and flung themselves down on the sand. They took off their shoes to feel sand between their toes. On one side of the beach were mangroves, on the other they could see a path up a cliff.

Ayesha decided to go for a swim. She shed some of her clothes. Oh well, I'll take them all off, she thought, what do I care? I don't think Jihad will do anything to me. Totally naked and with her back to Jihad, she ran straight into the sea, shouting wildly and waving. Up to her knees in water, she heard Jihad padding over the sand, and the swish as he entered the water. What would he do?

She turned and started splashing him. He was naked too. They played in the water, diving into it to get away from each other and laughing. It was such a relief.

When they were wading out, Jihad noticed men coming through the mangroves.

'Quick, grab your clothes and we'll make a run for the forest.'

They quickly disappeared behind some bushes and kept going, not risking discovery by the men.

They came to a farm again, and a farmer saw them and called out. They began to run away, but the farmer shouted, 'I'll help you.'

Still fearing that they might be turned in to the jihadists, Ayesha and Jihad hesitated. The farmer was walking towards them, and called, 'I won't harm you. What are you doing here?'

He had reached them. They explained briefly what they were doing. He said, 'I'm a good Muslim. I'll help you.'

They went with him to his house and had showers and a meal. The farmer was able to phone the police and army. Not long after, they heard a helicopter.

Ayesha panicked. She said to Jihad, 'Come outside, I want to talk to you in private.'

They went out the back and she said, 'I believe it could be a trick. How else could he get us to stay there while he arranged for us to be captured? I'm not staying one minute more.'

'I've got no option but to remain with you,' said Jihad.

They walked fast to get behind a row of trees leading to the forest before the farmer would wonder what they were doing. When out of view, they ran. They continued their journey through the thickest jungle, where the farmer was unlikely to follow them. They had become skilled at surviving in the jungle.

So it was that they eventually arrived at a beach again. Exploring along the back of the beach, they discovered caves.

'We can live in a cave,' said Ayesha with delight. 'We can catch fish to stay alive and find water and other food in the forest. We could live like this forever.'

'I'm not thinking of doing that.'

'Me neither! What do you miss most?'

'The food. What do you miss?'

'A comfortable bed.'

After taking a dip in the sea, they went to look for food in the forest and to gather grass for their beds. They lost count of the days they lived like this without seeing any people or hearing helicopters or planes.

'It's easy to live in a cave in a hot country,' said Ayesha. 'People in northern countries always had to think about how to stay alive and advance themselves.'

She asked Jihad what he wished to do with his life.

'I want to earn enough money so I can be independent of my parents and don't have to live at home being fed by them. And so I can support my own family in the future. What do you want?'

'I hope to become truly literate and do something for my people. I would teach the children to read and write. If I can find a man to love, I will marry.'

Soon, Jihad said, 'I'd like to continue our journey. We need a boat to go by sea.'

'I've thought about it. We should try to make a raft out of sticks. We don't have a saw to use on thicker pieces of timber. We would lash the sticks together with vines. Your knife might be useful for vines.'

They went to search for sticks and vines and bring them back to the beach. When they had a good pile, they lined up a platform of sticks and started to weave vines between them and tie the ends. Eventually, they had a reasonable-looking raft of the size that two people could sit on.

Ayesha took the raft into the water to see if it would float. It did. Then she and Jihad tried sitting on it, and it sank downwards, tipping and bending this way and that as they moved.

'It feels unstable,' said Ayesha. 'We will have to build it up, with more layers of sticks, to be thicker and stiffer. But the vines are coming apart.'

They collected more sticks and went on building the raft. But the vines were unravelling.

Ayesha said, 'What we need is a long straight log of

wood – I've seen them around. It would float and we could ride astride it and paddle with our hands. Or hold onto it and paddle with one hand. Can you actually swim? – because you must be able to.'

'No, I can't.'

CHAPTER 26

Ayesha said, 'I'll teach you to swim. I'm a good swimmer and I wouldn't let you drown. Did you know you can easily float on your back in the water with your arms and legs spread out?'

Jihad shook his head.

'I'll show you how to do it. Also, you could learn to dog paddle.'

She took Jihad into the water on a calm day. First, she taught him to float. It was easy, just a matter of realizing you could do it. Then she got him to lie on his front with her arm under his chest, and made him dog paddle, which he had seen her do before. Gradually, she removed her arm, while saying, 'Keep going, keep going.' He was off on his own before he noticed she wasn't standing beside him any more. He practised this with her always present in the water, until he felt confident.

They went into the forest to search for a log. It wasn't hard to find one, but could they move it? It was covered with vines and vegetation and had partially sunk into the ground.

'Look,' said Ayesha, 'a giant earthworm!' It was coming out of the ground onto the log, about a metre long.

Jihad used his knife to free the log. Scorpions ran out from under it and they kept moving their feet away from them. They saw some big slugs which they swallowed whole without a thought of how disgusting they were. They would have to lever the log out of the ground. They managed to roll it a little. Now they tried to lift or slide it. Nothing budged. Ayesha sat down and put her face in her hands.

'I'm tired. I'm going to rest a bit.'

Jihad disappeared into the forest for a while and came back with two very strong sticks.

'We can use these for levers.'

'We need paddles too. Look for pieces of wood that would do.'

Ayesha got up to help him. At last, they both returned with paddles to choose from.

'We'll have to inch the log along with the levers,' said Ayesha.

Struggling for a time, they moved the log a little along the ground, with the log pointing to the sea. It was taking an eternity, it seemed. They found flat leafy branches to pave its way better. At the edge of the sand, it was more difficult. But they persevered and reached the water.

Ayesha circled the log in two places with the vine and tied it in a sort of knot. Then she formed the remaining stems into two loops and attached the ends to the circles. They had handles! They were ready to push the log into the water. It was fairly calm, without waves. They launched it.

'Hang on to the log!' cried Ayesha, as Jihad took the front position. They started to paddle.

'We want to go north-west,' said Ayesha, 'and I

believe the current is mainly south-east around the islands, so it will be hard work, and slow. But the current is not strong as water gets banked up by the islands.'

'How do you know all this?'

'I've learnt it from the Bajau. They have to know about currents and all behaviours of the sea.'

Ayesha saw that the sun was now setting in the west. She pointed to the north-west direction they should aim for.

In a while, she said, 'Slide off the log and see if you can float the way I taught you.'

Keeping hold of his handle, Jihad slid off without hesitation, tried it, and it worked.

'Now kick your legs, and you will propel the log along.'

He tried it.

'Now let go the handle and do backstroke.' She demonstrated with her arms. 'Don't be afraid.' Hope he doesn't float away from me.

He tried it, but soon stopped and grabbed the handle again.

'Turn over and do a dog paddle, kicking your legs at the same time.' She demonstrated with her arms again.

'Oh, no,' he said. But he did it.

'Swim harder. You're sliding back towards me.'

He reached for the handle and put his leg over the log. He'd had enough.

'From what you know, you'll be able to save yourself,' said Ayesha. 'The next thing I'm going to tell you is, there are sharks in this water.'

'We'll get eaten alive!'

'No, remember your knife. If you're attacked, stab the shark in the eye. If one attacks me, I'll go for its eyes with my fingers. It'll go away.'

They went on paddling.

'Our clothing will cover us well from the sun in the day,' said Ayesha. The sun had nearly set. 'Our brown skin is a sufficient protection.' Her people often used a homemade sun protection cream.

It was a calm, clear night. Ayesha could see the north star just above the horizon. If it were cloudy, they wouldn't be able to see it.

'We've got a long journey ahead,' she said, trying to keep Jihad awake. 'Maybe a plane or helicopter will see us. They might already be searching for us. Sometimes, we heard a helicopter when we were escaping.'

If we both fall asleep it will be disastrous, she thought. Still holding the vine handle, she twisted it to circle it around her wrist. She called Jihad to do the same.

They continued this way through the night without mishap. Somehow, they managed to doze on and off while still paddling and without falling off the log. Ayesha remained aware of her situation all night and immediately awoke if she became unbalanced.

In the morning, she noticed a boat in the distance. I hope no boats come close to us, she thought. We would look pretty funny sitting on a log and we don't want to explain anything. The boat stayed away.

'Our position in relation to other islands seems much the same as last night,' she said. 'It's deceptive. I remember being on a motorboat and thinking we weren't making much progress, but we were.'

It became very monotonous. They had some food in their pockets, which was getting used up. No drinkable water.

At a much later time, Jihad noticed a grey shadow in the sea that appeared to be following them.

He said, 'I think there's a shark to the right of the log.'

'Can you pull your legs out of the water?'

'This is going to be a balancing act!'

'And tiring.'

The log became a bit unstable when they both straightened their legs out in front of them. It was awkward. They gripped the log sufficiently with their heels. The grey shadow gradually slipped away.

'We'll have to land on an island to find water,' said Ayesha.

But the shark returned. It swam up close to their legs, as if it were sniffing them. Jihad drew his knife but couldn't reach its eyes. Ayesha was looking straight into the shark's wide-open mouth. Any minute, it would rear up and push her off the log. I must jam something down its throat. Jihad's knapsack was on his back facing her. She tore her it off his shoulders and shoved it into the shark's mouth, leaning forward to push it well into its throat. Both my arms are inside its mouth, she thought with horror. She saw the flash of the blade of Jihad's knife as it narrowly missed her arm and cut into the shark's eye. Bleeding profusely and with its throat blocked, the shark turned and swam away.

It was no trouble to locate an island. Soon, they drew in to the shore. It seemed to be deserted. Because of the jungle nearby, there was water on the leaves to lick off. The found a small trickle going to the sea. They had finished all their bush food.

Sitting on a rock, Jihad said, 'We'll have to hunt for food again.'

'Getting used to the lifestyle?'

He didn't answer. Then he suddenly got up and was disappearing into the jungle.

Ayesha called, 'Don't get lost.'

After she had rested, she went in search of Jihad, as he hadn't returned. She walked in the direction she'd seen him go, calling for him as she went. There were roots on the ground trying to trip her up. I must remember the direction back to the log.

Sometime later, she heard groaning. She followed the sound and came upon Jihad lying on the ground with a vine twisted around his ankle.

'Couldn't you have shouted?' she said.

'I hit my head on a rock when I fell and I think I passed out for a while.'

Ayesha freed his foot, but he was complaining of pain.

'Stand up and see if you can limp on it.' He could, but the ground was rough.

'We'll get you back slowly. Look out for food as we go.'

They found some mushrooms. 'How do we know they're not poisonous?' said Jihad.

'We don't. They might be magic mushrooms, like a

drug.'

She carried the mushrooms in a pocket formed by her t-shirt. They would eat them back at the log. Fortunately, she remembered the way.

Out on the water again, they saw a boat. This time, the boat came towards them.

'Are you all right?' a man called.

'Yes, thanks.'

The man was now close enough to see they were astride a log.

'What happened to you?'

'We had an accident with our boat but swam ashore.'

The man revved up his engine and went off, leaving the log riding his wake. Then another boat was coming towards them. When it was close enough, Ayesha and Jihad saw that the men in it wore police uniforms.

'We escaped from the kidnappers,' said Ayesha, greatly relieved.

'We'll take you on our boat and to safety,' said one of the men.

They clambered into the motorboat with the helping hand of a policeman and found a seat. The boat sped towards the shore.

'We're going back to an island, not home,' said Ayesha.

'Some of us are getting off there first,' said the policeman.

CHAPTER 27

Gideon heard that Ayesha had disappeared from the convent. Someone there had been interviewed by police but they said they knew nothing as Ayesha hadn't informed them of anything, though her name was still on their books. It seemed like something unexpected had happened.

Gideon hired a boat ride to the stilt houses. After asking around, he located the place where Ayesha lived, and introduced himself as one of the students who had been in her class. Her father told him that they didn't know where she had gone, but they found her canoe in the water, undamaged, and without fish in it. As Ayesha could swim well, it was unlikely she had drowned. Someone must have taken her when she was on her way to the market early in the morning. Some other Bajau had gone in search of her too, without result.

'I plucked up courage and went to the police,' he said. 'They took it seriously and said they'd try everything to find her and notify the army.'

'I'll do anything I can too,' said Gideon.

When Gideon went to the police, they told him that Ayesha might have been kidnapped by the terrorists for a ransom. There were many such cases. Gideon consulted his father about the matter. 'I will have to raise the money for her.'

His father said, 'Give the police a chance to do something. They are striving to solve these cases. The troops will be sent in to find the terrorist's camp, but they change their location from time to time. The army has done a good job so far in catching these outlaws and rescuing the hostages. It would be extremely difficult for you to raise the funds and it would take time.'

Gideon felt unable to do anything about Ayesha on his own.

Chris had spent time driving around the islands by boat, drawing maps and marking landings. Finally, he thought he saw Ayesha with some police on a beach. There were caves at the back of the beach. He brought the boat to the shore, bouncing over the low surf. He felt it ground itself on the sand. He stepped out and pulled it up higher.

He shouted, 'Ayesha, Ayesha, is that you?' as he walked over the sand.

Ayesha screwed up her eyes. Was it Chris? Was it Gideon? *They've done it!*

When Ayesha recognized him, she called, 'Chris! You found us. How did you do it?'

'I took a boat around the islands looking for signs of life. I'm glad I've come across you at last, alive. Like searching for a pea in a haystack.'

'Thank you. I'm so grateful. We escaped from the kidnappers, and the police have also found us.' He reached her and she was too shy to give him a hug in front of the crowd.

'Now, down to business,' said a policeman. 'We need you to walk with us through the forest to help us find the kidnappers. We can't let you go off in a boat.'

They all looked amazed. 'Are we on the island where their camp is? We left it on our raft two days ago,' said Ayesha.

A policeman said, 'We are arresting you to make you come with us.' He stepped forward and put handcuffs on all of them.

'This is strange,' said Chris.

The police ignored him and pushed them into a line; then marched them off with confidence as if they knew where they were going. So now was beginning another long journey through the jungle.

'All these forest paths look the same,' said Ayesha, stumbling along.

'I think it's the same one,' said Jihad. 'They are close to finding the kidnappers.'

Being handcuffed, Ayesha found her balance over the rough ground was affected, and she risked falling and getting hurt.

She said to the police, 'Couldn't you take off the handcuffs so we can manage this difficult track without falling over – I often want to reach out and hold something. After all, you are armed.'

The policeman she spoke to discussed it with his fellow officers. They agreed to remove the handcuffs now that they were well away from the boats. They took away Jihad's knife. He was very upset about it.

'We'll return it when you leave.'

Chris said to Ayesha, 'Your family are well. They found your canoe. They believed you were okay because you are a good swimmer. They thought you had been kidnapped and went to the police. I went to the police too and they said they thought you might be being held for a ransom.'

'I'm so sorry this happened to you.'

To Jihad, Chris said, 'You were kidnapped too?'

'No, I joined the separatists earlier, but changed my mind when I saw Ayesha imprisoned in the hut. I had no idea she was going to be kidnapped. Her life was threatened.'

'I know. Do you think I could stay at home knowing that.'

Eventually, they reached the camp. It was the same one! The same hut. The police called to the kidnappers. At that moment, Ayesha and Jihad realized the police were some of the kidnappers in disguise. The so-called police went off to join the men in the camp.

How had she and Jihad managed to return to the same place on the raft? It must have been that the current in the sea was too strong and they were always slipping back without noticing it. At night, especially, they wouldn't have been aware of it.

The guard opened the door of the hut and Ayesha, Chris and Jihad joined Ove and Solange. Chris couldn't stand upright but had to bend his head.

'There are too many people in the hut now,' said the guard. 'We will have to get rid of one of you. Ove or Solange. We'll still get the same amount of ransom money from one of the couple. Or from the new prisoner.'

There was dead silence. Solange started to cry.

'I'll go,' said Ove.

'No, I will,' said Solange, sobbing.

The guard said, 'If you are going to fight about it, I will decide. Ove will die. Now.'

Ove seized Solange by the shoulders. He said, 'I have always loved you,' and kissed her.

She said, 'Goodbye, my darling.' She only saw him through tears.

Ayesha felt frozen to the ground. The guard tore Ove away and in a short time they heard a shot, footsteps going away from the hut and the body being dragged over the undergrowth. Faint voices and sounds of digging.

Solange was overcome with grief and inconsolable. Ayesha and Jihad were kind to her and, concealing their own suffering, maintained an atmosphere of love in support of her.

Solange said, 'Why do these men pray several times a day yet do things so evil and cruel?'

The kidnappers started to show they were bothered about Jihad being in the hut with two single women. He more than deserved to be there as a punishment, if not death, for his disloyalty in escaping. Jihad persuaded them he was a couple with Ayesha, and they were both taking care of Solange after her bereavement.

'If we kidnap more people, we'll have to shoot more,' said the guard.

Everyone was getting very tense and anxious now in the camp at large. Helicopters were repeatedly flying overhead. This went on for days.

'There's nowhere a helicopter could land near here,' said Ayesha.

'They're trying to sight the camp to send a message about it to the army,' said Jihad. 'We're going to be rescued.'

'I bet that will be a dangerous operation.'

One morning, the guard said, 'We're taking you, Ayesha, to our camp. If the militia storms the camp, we'll hold you in front of us and threaten to shoot you if they advance farther.'

Ayesha found herself in the jihadist's compound, being isolated and guarded. Food was brought to her. Without overhead shelter, she had to sleep on the ground like the others.

She said to the guard, 'My family could not possibly pay the ransom money you are asking. They are poor.'

He said, 'If we kidnap someone else, we'll shoot you first then. What about the rich students you know at the convent class? Their families have money. And the wealthy tourists? They can pay for you. We'll wait.'

The helicopters stopped flying overhead. It became very quiet for days. They know the spot and are advancing to it, Ayesha thought.

In the hut, one night, the prisoners woke up to a strange noise, like someone trying to breathe and stopping short. Then someone was quietly opening the door of the hut. By a tiny light, they saw a man in army uniform. 'Shh,' he said, holding a finger to his lips.

'The guard,' whispered Jihad.

'He's dead.'

'Ayesha's not here.'

'Where is she?'

'They took her to the men's camp and will threaten to shoot her if you attack.'

'Is there a married couple here?'

'They shot the husband and another man is here.'

'Remain here until we tell you to come.'

Jihad heard the soldier whispering to others. A short time later, the hut inhabitants heard a great deal of shooting from the men's camp. A woman screamed. They looked at one another in alarm.

'She might not survive this,' Chris said.

'Some soldiers may die or be wounded,' said Solange.

They heard noises like people crashing through the forest.

CHAPTER 28

Ayesha was woken up and dragged roughly by some jihadists into the forest, moving very fast. She screamed from shock but immediately had her mouth and hands bound and was told they would shoot her if she made a noise. Shots rang out at the camp.

Ayesha's group were on an uphill climb through dense vegetation. The men seemed to know where they were going. At last, they reached the top of a hill, where the ground opened out.

A man said, 'There is a cliff here above the creek. If you cause any trouble we'll push you over the cliff onto the rocks. You won't survive.'

The men talked quietly about what to do and where to go next. Two younger men were consigned to guard Ayesha and they took her to the cliff edge. She sat down to rest.

Suddenly, there was shooting as soldiers crashed into the main group of men. The two with Ayesha pulled her up.

One said to the other, 'Quick, we'll run.'

The other said, 'Over you go,' and they both pushed her over the cliff. She was falling.

She only thought of Dido. I'm coming to you, Dido, down there in the rocks. You won't be lonely any more.

She was floating down through the water, past seaweed and fishes to where he died. Her hands trailed over the rocks as she looked for the entrance to Heaven. She saw Dido and reached out her arms to embrace him. She would be with him now for ever.

Back at the hut, soldiers came to collect Jihad, Chris and Solange.

'We must make a speedy getaway up the track,' said a soldier. 'Do exactly as we tell you as it is still dangerous. Some of our men were killed. Some separatists ran into the jungle and may attack us as we return.'

'What happened to Ayesha?' said Chris. 'The girl who was taken from us to the men's camp.'

'I don't know. She may be coming with other soldiers.'

In no time, the hostages were ordered into a column and began to proceed along the track in the dark, not knowing whether Ayesha was alive or dead. They were walking along a route that was becoming familiar to them.

Soldiers were stalking along the creek below the cliff. They saw a body lying in the sand banks. When they investigated it, they discovered it was a woman. They removed the bindings to her hands and mouth. She was unconscious but still alive. They needed a stretcher and feared to move her because of injuries being made worse by it. They fashioned something from sticks and their own clothing. It didn't look strong enough.

At the same time, the woman stirred and called, 'Dido,

Dido.'

A soldier said, 'Are you all right? Can you sit up?'

She slowly pulled herself up, groaning. 'It hurts. I feel dizzy.'

'If you can manage it, we'll carry you on someone's back, in turn.'

'Where are Chris, Jihad and Solange?' She started weeping.

'They're walking back with the other soldiers. Are you Ayesha?'

'Yes. What about the kidnappers?'

'Dead or gone into hiding. We're still trying to round them up.'

A soldier squatted down with his back to her, telling her to put her arms around his shoulders. 'Hold tight to my jacket.'

As he stood up and wrapped his arms around her legs, she cried in pain but still clung on.

'We're in business,' he said to the other soldiers.

They turned to walk back to the main group. 'We'll try to catch up with them on the route home.'

It was painful jolting along the track, but Ayesha knew at least she had no serious injury. Every now and then, she was given some water and the carrier was changed. It seemed ages, over and around the tree roots, never catching up with the others.

Still trying to find out about Ayesha, Jihad asked a soldier just behind him about her.

'I don't know anything,' he said. 'I'll pass the

message down.'

A message came back that Ayesha was injured but managing to travel with them at the back. Then, after an interminable time, a message was returned that Ayesha wasn't with them, but the soldiers were searching for her. Maybe it was like Chinese whispers.

At last, the whole convoy of soldiers with the hostages arrived at the beach. Ayesha's group were the last in. Ayesha had been sleeping and woke up sitting on the sand. There was Chris, Jihad and Solange looking at her with relief.

'I'm okay,' she said. She tried to rise and fell back. Pain and stiffness.

A soldier squatted down and said, 'Don't worry. You're going back in the helicopter.'

The helicopter was parked nearby. Chris's boat was still grounded on the shore. The soldiers were permitted to sit on the ground and take a rest.

The leader of the soldiers said, 'Ayesha, Solange and Jihad, together with a handful of soldiers, will board the helicopter to return to town. The remainder of the troops will stay to flush out enemy loose in the forest.'

Chris bent down and gave Ayesha a hug. 'I'll have to take my boat back. We'll meet up again soon.'

Jihad climbed into the helicopter with Solange and gave Ayesha a hand up while a soldier steadied her from below. Chris went to start up the motorboat and was off. While he still had the boat, he drove it out to the stilt houses and told Ayesha's family about her release from capture.

In hospital, Ayesha felt elated about her rescue from the kidnappers. She had sustained no serious injuries. Her mother came. As soon as Ayesha saw Ma, she began to cry.

Mum sobbed too as she gave her a big hug and said, 'Ayesha, we're glad and relieved to have you back. Chris told us about you.'

'Mum, I'm so happy to see you again. I don't have much wrong with me, but I'm here for rest and observation.'

'Dad is unwell and not working at present. He just seems very tired.'

'He never takes a holiday. How are you off for fish?'

'We have enough food for now. I'm going to the market every day. I tell Gran to mind Dad while I'm away.'

While Ayesha was recovering in hospital, a government official came to ask her questions in order to gather information that might help them deal with kidnappers in the future and prevent kidnapping. He said he didn't want to stress her, but Ayesha said no, she didn't mind recalling the events from her safe place, and she wanted to do anything that might help.

After she left hospital, she went straight home, someone dropping her off from their canoe. She went back to her usual work of selling the fish and getting the provisions.

Dad seemed to be dying and no medical intervention could save him. He seemed too young to die. The Bajau men always died much earlier than the women, working for their families so much.

Dad said, 'I worked hard all my life like a Bajau man should, supporting and feeding my family. I'm worn out now and need to die. It's the way things are.'

Ayesha said, 'Dad, you will see Dido again. You will be resting on the floor of the ocean where he is, and in Heaven. All is peace and calm down there. It's your home where you have spent all your life.'

'Dear Ayesha, I am gloriously happy about the way things are. I've had a wonderful life with you and my kind, good family. I look forward to my well-earned rest, lying peacefully there with God and my son. I could not wish for more than what I have. It is everything a human being could want.'

Ayesha said, 'Goodness and mercy all my days shall surely follow me, and in my father's house always my dwelling place shall be. I shall always be here, Dad. I'll go down into the sea and visit you and Dido.'

She had so much to do that, if Dad died, she would have to grieve another time. She knew it could happen any time, in a snap of the fingers, and she mightn't be there. Death was like that. If Dad died, who would catch the fish? She and Ma would have to get jobs on the land and abandon their reliance on fish, or they would have to learn to catch fish.

Dad said he had occasionally found a pearl when he was diving. He sometimes sold one but had put most away for the future. He told Ayesha to sell the pearls to pay for her classes at the convent. She could get a headstone carved for Dido to place on the rocks where he died. He was settling his affairs.

Gradually, Dad got better again.

Ma said, 'I believe Dad's grief at the thought of losing you to the kidnappers, combined with the stress of his usual work, was so great that it caused his illness.'

Of course, thought Ayesha, when he had lost Dido too. He must have thought he'd done something terribly wrong in his life.

CHAPTER 29

After Ayesha had settled herself at home again, she went to the drop-in centre hoping to see Chris. She didn't know where he lived, but he had left his address there. She went to his address. It was a room in a large building. No one answered the door. He has a job today, she thought. She sat on the floor in the corridor. It was already late afternoon.

When Chris turned up, he looked surprised but pleased to see her. They hugged.

'I'm already out of hospital and living at home again,' said Ayesha. 'I got your address from the drop-in centre.'

'I'm glad you did. Come into my room and talk,' Chris said, opening the door. He was dressed in workman's clothes, rather dirty. 'Sorry about the mess. I had a job today.'

Ayesha saw a table and two chairs and sat down while Chris made coffee.

She said, 'There is a place where we can go for therapy, they told me at the hospital. It's the same as where I went for drug counselling. The government pays for it, so I'm being treated like a real citizen. Chris, if you see the therapist, you will be able to join a discussion group of people who are suffering from a trauma. I know because I did it before to recover from the drug.'

'Yes, I know about the group. I will go when I don't have a job for the day. I do hard physical work in the day and am too tired at night. I desperately need to earn some money. I don't want to lose touch with you. I was hoping to see you at the drop-in centre, but I couldn't get there for lunch today. You must go for therapy on your own, as I can't guarantee I'll be there. I simply can't afford any more time to think about what happened. I think about it at night and it keeps me awake. But just seeing you makes me feel better!'

'I sleep badly too. I can never thank you enough for coming to find me.'

'No need. I want to protect you. I'll give you a key to my room and you can come here any time. Lock the door when you leave. I'll tell the landlady.'

'I would like it. I don't feel like going to my class at present, but I've gone straight back to my duties of selling the fish and taking home the provisions.'

She thought she would try out going to Chris's room and seeing what she felt like resting there for a while. When she went in, she sat down at the table and looked around. The window only showed part of a building and the sky. Chris's bed needed making, so she straightened out the sheets and blanket. Ma always made her bed at home. In his bedside table was a drawer. She pulled it out and found a pile of old bills, and pens and pencils.

I'll write something on the backs of the bills, she thought. A letter to Chris. He can read it when he gets home. She returned to the table, and wrote,

Dear Chris,

I often want to say more things to you, but we're both so busy. Well, you are. You are probably tired too. You tried to rescue me and risked your own life.

You are my angel and I am your princess (so I think in a fanciful sense – I am my dad's princess, really.) You're always nice and personable. A gentleman in workman's clothing. You understand a person's weaknesses because you had to suffer cancer. You warned me about the drug and encouraged me not to take it and supported me when I was giving it up. Thank you for all this.

I often want to talk with you when you are not present, and this is the way. I appreciate you more than you know. I value your friendship. What can I do for you?

Ayesha thought it might help her to do hard physical work like Chris and be too tired to think at night. What work could she do? Well, she could dig a vegetable garden for someone again, walking from door to door asking for this work, and being paid for it.

She went to Noor's place and found out that the students all knew about how she had been rescued.

'How are you doing?' Noor said. 'Being kidnapped must have been awful. I feel so inadequate in comprehending it.'

'I am well, and will be having therapy,' said Ayesha, not wanting to make much of it. 'I don't want to give you all the details.' Noor would have no idea just how awful it was.

Noor said Tomasin, Jake and the twins had returned

to the countries they had come from.

'Jake went with Tomasin to America, but I believe he came from England.'

She was going to take over Sunny's project of housing street children at night in the disused factory, as her father had had an extension of time at the university. The girls at the refuge were in danger of being trafficked for sexual exploitation. Even boys were.

'I'm looking for extra help from the remaining students and anyone else. Also local government. Can I call on you? Later, when you have recovered.'

'Of course. I want to go back to my garden there and try growing vegetables.'

When Ayesha went for therapy, she was seen by Zoe again.

Zoe said immediately, 'You are always welcome to come back here. You know that. You may have a delayed reaction to your kidnapping – weeks, months or years.'

'Do you know what has happened to Solange?'

'She went back to her parents in another country.'

'Poor Solange. I never said goodbye.'

'You feel part of a group, don't you?'

'Yes. Jihad and Chris too. I've been in touch with Chris. I don't know Jihad's address.'

'We've contacted both of them about coming for therapy. Would you like to talk about your experience?'

'I don't know what to say. I feel very happy to be home, and still alive. I keep thinking about it at night and can't get to sleep. My father has nearly died. I feel a need to grieve for losses, but I have so much on my plate that

I've put it off till another time. I'll do it gradually. Do you think that's normal?'

'Yes, people often act like that in these circumstances. Do you have any nightmares?'

'Sometimes, like almost being eaten by a shark, or starving and dying in the jungle. In the day, I'm a bit tired and numb, but I don't mind. I don't want to do anything much. I notice I feel frightened of the police if I'm out and about. The kidnappers tricked me by wearing police uniforms.'

'You could write down in the day what you are recalling at night. This might help you deal with what you went through. Or at least help you to sleep – tell yourself at night that you've written it all down and don't need to think about it again. But you still might think about it. Old fears and anxieties may return to haunt you.

'I'll see you again. I'd like you to join a discussion group we have of people who are recovering from a trauma. Could I put your name down for this group once a week?'

'Yes.'

Zoe told her a day and time to come.

When Ayesha met up with Chris again, she immediately said, 'You don't talk to me enough. Why is that? Be honest.'

'I'm a bit over-awed by you. Look, I loved getting your letter. I am your friend indeed. I'm not so fantastic as all that. But still.'

'I really meant what I said. I'm a good person too.'

'I want to say, I once had a relationship with a woman

before.'

'Did you feel automatically that she was the one?'

'Pretty much. It is so wonderful, and you have nothing to compare it with.'

'That's what I felt about Gideon. My whole being was overcome by it. Why didn't your love last?'

'We wanted to do different things, which interfered with each other's lives.'

'That was true of me too. But really it was because we didn't match each other.'

She wrote next time in Chris's room, *I was saved from becoming pregnant with Gideon's child in a car by the police arriving. I was saved from being readdicted to a drug by the pandemic because the dealers disappeared under threat of being shot by police or fear of the disease. I have been saved from death at the hands of the kidnappers by you and the army. I didn't deserve it but was saved by the grace of God. Now I appreciate every day of my life more. Life is always better than nothing, even if you are reviled. I owe it to God to lead a better life. As Jesus said, "By their fruits you shall know them".*

I haven't told you about Jihad. He nearly raped me once, but I managed to put him off because I called his name and reminded him we'd spoken before. When I saw him again, I said I'd turn the other cheek and still be his friend, as that is what the true Christians do. I don't think he made the jihadists kidnap me, but I'm sure they knew of me through him.

When he had a change of heart and came to free me from the hut in the jungle, I think my turning the other cheek at the earlier time influenced his decision to do that. I'll never know. As we slashed our path through the jungle, he looked after me and never took advantage of me. So I don't harbour any hard feelings towards him now, and I don't think about the near rape much any more. I think he was a rather foolish young man.

When Ayesha saw Chris next, he said, 'What you wrote about Jihad blew my mind. I think you've done well to be free of him if that's what it is.'

'Yes. I don't want anything to do with him now. We don't have to get on with everyone in the world. Live and let live.'

If she continued to write to Chris, she thought, their relationship would deepen.

Chris's father had decided to retire, and hand over the farm to Chris. His mother and sister would still work on it, but his sister was planning to marry. Ayesha said she could help on the farm, while still doing her duties at home. They wouldn't be able to go to the full-time secondary school course at the convent she was interested in, but Chris said there were technical college courses they could do part-time, partly school subjects and partly technical ones. He was sure they wouldn't discriminate against Ayesha.

Chris said, 'You know I love you, Ayesha. I told you before. Would you marry me?'

'I will. But I have to think about how my life would be.'

'I'm so happy. We won't rush then.'

'Really, I don't want to live in a flat in town. I'd prefer to live out in a stilt house.'

'I would come and live with you if you'll have me.'

'Oh, we could have Gran and Grump's room. Gran won't mind having my room.'

She wanted to stay at home and help Ma look after Gran. If Dad died, she would learn to dive and catch fish. She was strong. She would become a hunter warrior princess.

You have no idea how nice it is to listen to the sea at night, Ayesha wrote to Chris, *slurp, slurp, as it slaps and sucks at the house in a regular rhythm. It puts you to sleep. The seagulls tap on the window in the morning to wake you up. We could live on a houseboat of our own and sail it to other countries. You could find casual building work. I would do the cooking and look after our children. We would always have fish to eat. I want to think what our future would be. But we ought to be more ambitious than that.*

She imagined she became pregnant with Chris's child. She would give birth to the child at her home, like the Bajau did. The baby would be a boy, like the boy of Princess Ayesha who started their tribe.

She would call her son 'My little prince' and would name him Prince. No one could revile him with a name like that. She would make sure he knew about Dido and where he was buried. Her parents would love him. He would lead his family into a new future.

She wanted to teach Prince to read and write when he was old enough. She would teach other children too – maybe she would start a school. Yasmin would marry Odin and have children. She would teach the children not to be afraid of other people outside the Bajaus, but to be cautious though. Not to feel put down by them, but to aspire to achieve the best in life. And always to remember their roots. Maybe the government would recognize her teaching and pay her for it.

She was hoping to set up a foundation to educate her people. She would make enquiries and begin to set it up. She would ask friends to donate to a fund to help the Bajau. They would say they would when they had enough money to do so. She would write a memoir of her life, a book about her tribe to raise people's consciousness about their plight. There were black people in America, or anywhere, who would understand her.

She had felt afraid to go on to Western education because she thought people would always discriminate against her. She'd have to struggle and wouldn't do as well as others. She could try for a scholarship to go to America. Would they accept who she was? She wouldn't be lonely if Chris came with her.

In her tribe, there was always love and respect. It was rewarding. She could become a sister, like Sister Rosa, if she wished. They needed help with people in trouble.

One day, Ayesha bumped into Jihad in a supermarket, where he was putting goods on a shelf. He told her he was engaged.

'I behave well, or my fiancée says she will leave me if I don't,' he said with a twisted grin.

He said he had worked in a storeroom, but now had a

better job in the supermarket, with prospects of career advancement.

Ayesha was glad for news of Jihad, glad for him, and felt her life had moved away from his.